Lone Star

Dawn L. Lubertowicz

SONGS

Lone Star by Dawn L Lubertowicz and Olivia Banta

Small Town Love by Olivia Banta and Dawn L. Lubertowicz

I'm Your Lone Star by Dawn L. Lubertowicz

Sweet Sweet Katelyn by Dawn L. Lubertowicz and Olivia Banta

CONTENTS

PROLOGUE

Fate can be both kind and cruel. When I saw a face from my past, standing at the gas station, I thought I was the luckiest man in the world. A second chance... I really thought I had one until fate decided to be the two-faced bitch that she is and took my chance away. Fate is just like everyone else, it likes to tease you with something before it's ripped it away from you. But then, it decides to give you a little something. Something to remember your second chance for a lifetime and it hurts every single second of your life, each beat of your heart.

This is the story of how fate can be both kind and cruel...

-Luke

CHAPTER ONE

Katelyn rushed through the apartment, leaving drawers on the floor with items broken and a mirror smashed over the dresser. Katelyn brushed the hair back that had been swinging into her viewpoint every time she looked down, flinching when she touched the sensitive part on her eye. She tried to cover up the black eye, but knew it was still there. Quickly, she threw some items in the only baggage she had, not caring if they were folded or not. She needed to get out before it was too late. Looking around one last time, she tried to keep her composure. Shaking her head, she stopped zoning out and going through all the memories she had here. Rushing out the door, she didn't bother to look back as it slammed behind her. Even the muffled sound of a cellphone going off didn't stop her as she ran down the stairs. Tears streamed down her face as she tried to stay strong, but she knew her mind and body couldn't take anymore.

***

Katelyn stared out the bus' window, watching the world she knew for so many years disappear as the sun started to set. Her body felt so exhausted from everything, but she just couldn't shut her eyes. Something in the back of her mind made her believe she was still in danger.

Even though, there wasn't much to look at, she continued to keep her gaze fixated outside. Her mind kept going through everything, trying to figure out what happened.

"What did I miss?" she asked herself.

***

Katelyn's muscles were stiff when she moved, as the bus started to slow down. Her eyes widened as she realized where they were. Looking around, she couldn't believe that the bus route took them through her old hometown. The shuffling of feet made her aware that the bus driver was standing at the front.

"Okay, everyone, if you need a potty break, I suggest you do it now, as you know, the restrooms in the back are out of order," the bus driver announced.

Katelyn exhaled sharply, not liking how this bus trip had turned unfortunate. She didn't want to get off the bus, but could feel her bladder was about to burst if she didn't, and waited for most of the people to get off before exiting the bus. Quickly looking around and over her shoulder, she knew those habits were hard to break. Keeping her head down, she went into the gas station, hoping no one she knew would see her here.

Almost crashing into someone, she looked up in time to see them looking at her strangely. Exhaling again, she realized that there was a long line for the bathrooms. Leaning up against the wall, she decided to wait it out. Tapping her foot, she kept her head down. Her stomach was doing twists and turns as she continued to hope and pray no one would recognize her.

Eventually, it was her turn to use the restroom, and she quickly ran in before the other person was completely out of the doorway. As she sat on the toilet seat, she began to rock, and wrapped her arms around her stomach to try to calm it. Letting out a shaky breath, she closed her eyes to get her mind to stay focused on one thing instead of a million things.

***

The bus driver came in and looked around.

"Last call!" he shouted, before exiting the store, and everyone began to pile out so they wouldn't miss the bus.

***

Katelyn splashed some cold water on her face before looking at herself. She couldn't believe the image looking back at her. It was not what she used to look like. She used to be radiant and had color. Looking back at her was a ghost of a shell that was battered and worn down. She carefully dried her face so she wouldn't remove the foundation hiding the black eye. She didn't need people asking about it.

***

Katelyn walked out, fixing her messed up bun. Her head sprung up and her eyes went wide, hearing air releasing and then a motor going. Running out the door, she threw her arms down harshly.

"No!" she screamed after the bus.

Dust and dirt kicked up as the bus left the gas station. Her hand slapped her forehead, she couldn't believe that the bus had left her behind. She didn't know what she would do as everything she owned was still on the bus.

Turning around slowly, she went back into the gas station and hoped there was some help in there. Walking up to the counter, she didn't recognize the clerk and was glad he wouldn't recognize her. She gripped the counter edge to keep calm.

"Excuse me, can I use your phone?" she asked quietly.

The clerk looked up from stocking cigarettes before answering. "Sure."

As he went to grab the phone, she looked out the window, hoping that the bus driver had realized she wasn't on it and turned back around to pick her up. Her nervousness got the best of her as she started to tap all of her fingers on the counter. Slowly, looking back where the clerk stood, she realized he was, arching his brow at her. She could tell she must look suspicious by the way she was acting, but she was having a bad day. The clerk eventually handed over the cordless phone for her to use.

"Thanks," she said softly.

The clerk left her as she turned around to try to get some privacy. She stared at the phone and had no idea who to call. Her parents were both deceased and she wasn't going to call the asshole she left for help. This was a new beginning for her. So who was she going to call? At that moment, she made herself laugh a little, not only because she realized she had no one, but the fact that *Ghostbusters* echoed in her head.

Letting out a sigh, she turned around and handed the phone back. She didn't have anyone left that would save her after all the bridges she had burnt leaving here. The clerk took the phone back cautiously as if she was about to attack him.

"I'm sorry to bother you, but do you know when the next bus comes?" she asked, timidly.

"Oh, not for another week or so," he laughed, showing a smile.

Katelyn's mouth just hung open. The clerk cleared his throat as his smile faded.

"Sorry, miss, but it's rare when they drive through here," he apologized, rubbing the back of his neck.

"It's okay," she said, before turning around

She slowly walked out of the store, still in shock. What was she going to do now? She stared at the ground before her, trying to concentrate on her feet so she wouldn't have a meltdown.

"Katelyn?"

Katelyn stopped in her tracks and slowly looked up where the male voice came from. Standing before her was a man with brown hair and baby blue eyes which at that moment reminded her of puppy eyes. His jaw hung open as he was surprised as well. He wore a flannel shirt opened, revealing a white tank shirt and his blue jeans were held up by a brown belt wrapped snuggly above his hips.

Katelyn didn't know what to do. All she could do was stare at a face she hadn't seen for years. The last time she saw him was when she left this town for something better. Her body began to shake, but she contained herself, not wanting to fall apart in front of him.

"Luke?" she asked quietly.

***

Luke couldn't help but smile. He thought for sure he must have fallen off the tractor harder than he thought when he saw his childhood love standing before him. He examined her and couldn't believe she was actually standing right in front of him. Of course, he noticed she looked a little different, she was a different color and style, but he would recognize her anywhere. Swallowing hard, he didn't know what to do or say as he had been dreaming of this moment since she left. He slowly walked toward her so he wouldn't spook her. Laughing inside his head, he couldn't believe what he was thinking as she wasn't a shy horse.

"Katelyn... is that really you?" he asked, still not sure.

A small smile appear on her face, but her hazel eyes didn't light up as they used to do when she smiled. Usually her smiles were big and would light up the whole room. This smile was barely shining, almost as dim as candlelight. Her body also showed the stress she had been through as she appeared thinner and lacked her normal radiant color. His heart ached, wondering what had happened to the darling girl he once knew.

He was only inches from her, just standing there still shocked that she was there. He couldn't seem to remove his eyes from her, and his arms wanted so much to wrap her up and hold onto her tight so she wouldn't leave again. He finally had to shake his head to get out of the trance.

"So...how have you been?" he asked, his voice shaking.

She shook her head as his smile grew, knowing she must have been in the same trance.

"Good... I'm okay," she answered, looking around and wrapping her arms around herself.

Luke's smile disappeared when she wouldn't look him in the eye. He had never had such a conversation with her without her eyes locked with his. He thought he saw something when her neck moved, but her shirt was hiding it well.

"Well, that's good to hear," he said, looking down.

Luke hated the awkwardness between them as he kicked some dirt and pebbles around with his boot. He had never felt like this before with her. They were always comfortable with each other, but she seemed to be a ghost of her former self. Looking back at her, she was trying to hide herself more from him. He hated this as he knew something had happened to make her act like a scared little animal.

"So, what brings you back here?" he asked, wanting the conversation to continue.

"Um… well…" Katelyn looked around before looking at the ground. "Just driving through," she finally answered.

Luke looked around the dirt parking lot and the only vehicle he saw was his silver '69 Dodge Charger with a black racing strip on the hood, parked at the gas pump. He was getting gas when he spotted her coming out and shouting. Then she headed back in and came back out as he was heading inside to see if it was really her. He kept eying her suspiciously until finally she threw her arms down.

"Okay! I'm not driving through! My bus left me behind!" she explained loudly, close to crying.

"Hey, it's okay," Luke reassured her, wrapping her up in his arms and rocking her.

He couldn't help but smile as it felt good to hold her again. He took a quick sniff of the nape of her neck, but realized she didn't smell the way she used to. Pulling her tighter against him, he tried to stop himself whisking her away and taking care of her. It appeared she could use some rest and care. She was the first to push away as he tried his best to keep her in his arms. Her hands on his chest made his heart stop as they locked eyes.

"Don't worry about me, I'll just wait here for the next bus," she said, with a forced smile.

He knew she was lying about being okay by the way her eyes spoke louder than her words. Shaking his head, he knew she would resist, but he would make sure she was okay.

"The hell you are," he said gruffly.

Her eyes widened and her body stiffened. He put on a smile to get rid of the fear that was forming in her eyes.

"You'll stay with me," he said, his heart fluttering.

Shaking her head, she pushed him farther away from her, his arms still out, hoping to bring her back.

"No, no… I can't."

"What? Are you going to camp out here and wait for the bus to come back," he teased, with a laugh.

She looked around before looking back at him. "I'll be fine," she said, with uncertainty in her voice.

Luke rolled his eyes, quickly picked her up, and threw her over his shoulder. He chuckled as it was like old times, especially when she started to kick and hit him.

"Luke! What are you doing?" she screamed.

"Apparently, kidnapping a stubborn mule," he answered, smiling.

"You do realize that kidnapping is a crime?"

"Not if I don't get caught... besides I need to save you."

In quick strides, they were on the passenger side of his Dodge Charger and he was opening the door. She continued her fit, but he enjoyed each hit and kick she gave him. It was definitely like old times. Once, he had her safely at the car, she placed her hands on either side of the door, making sure she wasn't completely inside. She acted like a cat trying to avoid getting into a tub filled with water. She glared at him, but he didn't take any insult from it, as he knew how to calm her down, but of course that would have to wait until later as he licked his chapped lips. His pants tightened a little as he recalled all those times of giving her such pleasure that their bodies were beyond exhausted.

Getting his mind back to the matter at hand, as she tried to escape he blocked her with his body and his arm out, his hand holding onto the door. She continued to glare at him, and he could see she was ready to fight.

"I'm not some damsel in distress that needs saving," she grated.

"Could have fooled me," he teased, with a big ass smile on his face.

She tried to go, but each time she tried to leave, his body was right there, like a wall, and blocked any escape. Even though it was pissing her off, he was enjoying feeling her body next to his which made his pants tighter.

Eventually, she grew tired and sat back on the seat. His smile faded into a frown as he was surprised how easily she gave up. Usually, she could go at this forever, but he could see she was exhausted. Crouching down, he examined her.

"Hey, are you okay?"

"Yeah." Her eyes opened after closing them for a moment. "Not as young as I used to be."

Luke really didn't like what had happened to her to make her like this. Removing his hands from holding onto the car door and frame, he held both her hands in his, looking down at them.

"I'm sorry, I was just teasing like old times," he apologized sincerely.

Looking up, he could see the fear in her eyes slowly going away.

"It's okay." She said softly, shaking her head. "It's been too long," she explained, looking in his eyes again.

"I'm sorry, Kate," he whispered, looking down.

He felt her fingers on his chin, lifting it. They locked eyes again.

"It's been a long time since I heard my name like that," she said, quietly.

A small smile appeared on her face and her eyes lit up. Luke couldn't help but smile as well.

"So, how about you take me up on my offer?" he asked, pleading in his voice.

Her smile grew slightly as she nodded in agreement. Luke smiled more and stood up.

"Good," he said.

He watched as she contemplated, looking over where she was originally at before looking at him.

"Thanks, Luke."

"No problem, darling," he said, with a southern drawl.

She let out a small laugh before sliding her legs into the vehicle. He smiled more, liking that he was able to make her smile with one of his sketches. She always loved it when he played a Southern gentleman and made sure to make the southern drawl exaggerated. Shutting the door gently, he made his way over to the driver's side and got in. As she put on her seatbelt, he couldn't remove his eyes from her as he examined her from top to bottom. His eyes returned to her face when she turned her head to look at him.

"Wow, I can't believe you still have this," she said, with shock in her voice.

"Yep, didn't have the heart to get rid of it," he explained with a smile.

Starting it up, he watched as her face lit up. He knew how much she enjoyed listening to the roar of the engine and then purr when it was idling. After she left, he couldn't get rid of it even though it held so many memories of them together.

"So, are you ready to head home?" he asked.

She laughed. "Home... it sounds so strange," she said, her face dropping as she stared out the windshield.

Luke's smile disappeared. He couldn't believe he made her this way again. He thought he was doing a fine job of making her feel comfortable. His mouth hung open as he was about to ask her what happened, but knew he better not ask. She appeared as if she wasn't ready to explain anything yet. Turning his head, he shifted the car in gear and drove away from the gas station with his second chance next to him.

***

Luke guessed that the quietness was getting to Kate, as she turned on the radio. He smiled when she started to sing along with the songs on the radio. She always had a beautiful voice. Her singing was interrupted by a yawn. He looked over and saw her rubbing her face, trying to stay awake.

"Hey, why don't you catch a quick nap?"

"No...I can't sleep until I feel safe."

He quickly looked over at her and wondered if she knew what she had said. He so wanted to ask her what was going on, but she seemed as if she'd been through a lot. She went back to her singing, distracting him from asking her the question. He continued to watch the road and listen to her singing.

So Heavenly...

During one of the long commercials, he felt eyes on him. He turned his head quickly to look over at her before looking back at the road.

"What's up, Kate?" he asked, as he read the questioning look on her face.

"I was just wondering how you're going to explain me to your family."

He did a quick laugh. "Well, Kate, my parents are dead, like yours."

He peeked over and saw her rolling her eyes.

"And I don't need to do any explaining to my sister, CindyLou," he explained.

"I know that. I meant your new family," she said, rolling her eyes again.

He looked over at her quickly, his mouth hanging open, and his eyes wide, before looking back at the road.

"New family?" he asked, with confusion in his voice.

"Yeah, you know, wife and children," she said harshly.

He looked at her for a moment and then back to the road, still not believing what he was hearing. In seconds, he started laughing so hard that he had trouble keeping the car on the road. She reached over to help steer, but he held up his hand.

"It's okay. I'm okay," he said, as the laughter faded.

Wiping the tears from his eyes, he had a big ass grin on his face.

"Oh, man, that's a good one, babe," he said.

Looking over again, he could see her brow was furrowed and placed a hand on her knee.

"I'm sorry, I didn't mean to laugh at you," he apologized.

"So, this whole time you never moved on?"

"Why?"

"So you could be happy."

"I was happy… I was with you." he said, looking at her.

Kate just stared at him with her mouth open before looking at the floor. Luke could feel the uneasiness between them as she kept shifting in her seat. Then a song came on to help salvage this moment. Luke smiled as *Closer* by Chainsmokers played on the radio.

Luke began to sing the first verse and looked over at her.

A smile slowly formed on her face.

"Come on, I know you know the words," he teased, shaking her knee.

He continued to sing with the radio waiting for her to join in. Then, when the female started to sing in the song, Kate joined in.

"You… look as good as the day I met… I forgot why I left you…" she sang along with the radio.

Luke smiled more as he continued to look over and enjoyed her singing again. Her voice was so amazing. Soon, they sang as a duet like in the song. Luke remembered all the times they had sung together like this. They would have been the next big thing if fate hadn't put a stop to it so many years ago. Kate grew tired of waiting and left to move on. But now fate was kind enough to bring her back to him so they could have each other again.

***

Kate couldn't help it as she kept singing with Luke. It was like old times. She didn't want to get in the car with him, but now that she was in it, she couldn't help but hope that maybe this was her second chance. As she continued to sing with him, she looked over at him as he looked back at

her.

I miss this…

As the song ended, he pulled off the main road, down a long, dirt road. Kate's stomach did flip flops as she recognized where they were going. It had been many years, but she recalled every bump on this road. As they hit every one, she counted as she used to when she was pleasuring him with either her mouth or hand to make sure she finished before they reached the last bump. She didn't want to get caught doing naughty things when his parents were roaming around the farm. It became a challenge for her to see how long he could last with her set of skills. She covered the smile on her face as her face became warm. All the memories of the moments together made her twitchy in her seat. From the corner of her eye, she saw Luke looking at her. She tried to hide what she was thinking, but imagined he knew what she was thinking, because he would look away and laugh.

As they pull up to the old farmhouse, she looked up at it. She couldn't believe it was still here. She thought for sure he would have moved on once she was gone, but he seemed to be holding onto the past. Startled, she placed a hand on her chest as she didn't hear him get out of the car and open her door. He held out his hand toward her, and she graciously took it as he helped her out of the car.

"Thanks," she said, looking at him from under her lashes.

She couldn't remove her eyes from his as they stood there. He finally broke the silence.

"So, do you have any clothes or anything?"

Her eyes widened before turning around.

"Shit!" she screamed.

She turned back to look at him.

"Everything I had was left on the bus."

"Hey, it's okay," he said, with concern in his voice.

Then he looked her up and down before a big smile appeared on his face.

"Besides, you always looked good either in my clothes or naked," he teased.

Kate laughed and it felt good to laugh this much. It had been so long since she had. She looked back at his face.

"Thanks, Luke."

"For what, my clothes or the compliment," he teased again.

"Both," she flirted back.

She didn't know what she was getting herself into, but it felt good to be flirty with Luke. The way he was looking at her was like old times, and her urges were an inferno now. Her eyes involuntarily flowed down his body to take in all of him before looking at his face again.

"Either sounds good to me," she said, seductively.

His jaw dropped open. She used her index finger to push on his chin to help shut his mouth.

"What, cowboy, wasn't expecting that?" she teased.

"Oh, hell no, darling, but I'm not going to complain," he said, with a smile.

She felt his body startle when she wrapped her arms around his neck and hugged him tightly.

"Thank you, Luke," she whispered in his ear.

She felt his smile on her skin as she made sure he didn't see the bruises on her neck. Most of them were covered, but the foundation could have wiped off. She didn't need him to worry too much about her. As he wrapped his arms around her tightly, she felt a familiar outline pressed against her. She smiled more, laughing inside her head, knowing that he surely did miss her by how his body was reacting to her.

"Wow, did you miss me or what?" she teased.

His body stiffened as she pressed her pelvic area harder against him.

He pulled away while clearing his throat. "Let's get you inside," he said, still embarrassed.

Kate laughed as his face was redder than a ripe tomato.

As he held open the door for her, she walked into a dark room. In an instant, he switched on the lights. She could see he had some updated items in the living room, such as a sectional with ottoman chair at the end, and a flat screen television. Other than those items, everything else looked the same. He quickly went past her and tried tidying up some stuff on the wooden coffee table. She covered her mouth to keep a laugh in as she could see it was cluttered with granola wrappers, chip bags, and mechanic magazines.

"Sorry, about the mess," he said, as he turned with the items in his arms.

Walking over, she placed a hand on his right cheek before planting a soft kiss on his left cheek. As she pulled away, she giggled when he dropped everything that was in his arms, smiling as she enjoyed the shocked look on his face.

"Oh… well…" he stuttered.

Kate kept the smile small and held the giggles back. He cleared his throat again and furrowed his brow.

"You must be hungry… I mean, are you hungry?" he asked, still stuttering.

"Yes," she answered simply.

"Okay, let's get something for you to eat," he said, with both hands behind him.

She started to walk, but he stopped her as a big grin appeared.

"No, let me make something for you. I imagine it has been a long day for you."

"Okay."

"How about you take a load off and watch some television," he offered, pointing with his outstretched hand.

"Okay, but you need any help, let me know," she said, before taking a seat on the couch.

***

Luke couldn't stop looking at her. He eventually had to shake his head to get focused on what he was doing. As he left the living room to go to the kitchen, he could hear her flipping through the channels. Once he was in the kitchen, he spun around a few times, not recalling where everything was, even though he had cooked many times in this kitchen. He started to grab pots and food items remembering how to cook. Laughing to himself, he still couldn't believe the power Kate had over him. When she was around him, his brain stopped working. She was the only girl to do that to him.

As he started to prepare the chicken to be baked, a smile appeared on his face, thinking this was his second chance with her. Finally, after begging and praying, his pleads and prayers were finally answered. Licking his lips, he wished he had kissed her when he first saw her, but he didn't want to spook her and have her run away again. His skin still tingled from where her soft lips had touched him.

Once he had everything he needed for the thawed-out chicken halves, he placed it in the oven, and whipped the towel over his shoulder. He figured, while the food was cooking, he would try his luck and kiss her just as he wanted to.

As he stepped into the living room, he stopped. He stared at Kate who had fallen asleep on the couch. He smiled, loving how she was sleeping peacefully now. He realized she must feel safe now, which made his heart flutter, knowing she was with him. Walking around the sectional, he crouched down to be at eye level with her. Brushing some of her hair back, he saw her lips. He so wanted to be like the prince and kiss her to awaken her as they did in the fairy tales that were read to them when they were younger.

Slowly standing, he slid his arms under her and lifted her up and gradually climbed the stairs so he wouldn't wake her. He would have placed her in a bed in the guest room, but it was being used for storage. So he took her down the hallway to his room. He softly placed her on the bed and covered her up as she rolled onto her side. Taking the towel from his shoulder, he noticed her wearing more foundation than he remembered. She wore makeup, but not the amount she had caked on. He slowly and gently wiped around her eye. Clenching his jaw, he tried to hold back his anger as he saw the bruising under the foundation. Moving her shirt a little, he was sure he saw bruising near her neck. Wiping some of the foundation away, he noticed the bruising resembled finger marks.

Letting out a sigh, he wished he knew what she had got herself into while she was gone. Throwing the towel over his shoulder again, he tried to calm down as he knew this wasn't the time to interrogate her about the bruises. Obviously, she was tired and needed to rest. Leaning down, he gently kissed her forehead before leaning closer to her ear.

"Goodnight, babe," he whispered.

Standing in the doorway, he turned his head and looked at her before leaving. He was scared that this was all a dream and when he woke up she would be gone. After making himself believe she was actually here, he made his way downstairs.

After putting the chicken in the fridge, he flopped on the couch, as he had in the past. After she had left, he hadn't dared sleep in the bed upstairs as it brought back too many memories. He had to get rid of the last couch they had as there were so many memories with that pull-out. The couch was the only thing he ever got rid of as he was certain she would return.

A smile spread across his face as he closed his eyes.

My second chance...

CHAPTER TWO

Kate stretched after throwing the blanket off her. She quickly sat up and thought she was back at her hell, but realized she was safe. She thought she would have gotten grief about not having breakfast ready, but she realized she didn't have to worry about that anymore. She made a slow walk to the bathroom as she remembered the layout of the old farmhouse. Looking at herself in the mirror, she realized that the bruising was showing through the thin foundation. On the counter, she spotted a plastic bag, opening it up, she found makeup in it. She smiled, holding up the foundation container.

"Oh, Luke," she said to herself as she started to reapply the foundation where she needed it the most. Luke was good to her, and she didn't want him to worry about the bruises on her body. Her stomach rumbled as she smelled breakfast being cooked downstairs.

"Just like old times," she said, smiling at herself in the mirror.

As Kate climbed down the stairs, she rubbed her face as she slowly made her way into the kitchen, where a wonderful smell of pancakes and bacon was coming from. Sitting at a little table, she held up her head with her hand, watching Luke cook.

"Morning, morning, morning," he said, turning to put some pancakes on her plate in front of her.

"Hmmm, why are you so cheery this morning?" she groaned.

Turned around, continuing to cook. "I'm not, just making sure to say morning for each morning you missed," he explained, turning back toward

her.

"What!" she said, fully awake.

***

Standing with a plate in his hand, he said, "Apparently, you needed it." He sat across from her. "You were sleeping like a rock. A stampede of cattle couldn't wake you up," he teased, with a smile.

His smile disappeared when he saw her poking a pancake with her fork. He reached across to encase her hand in his. She stared at his hand first before looking at him. He saw the fear in her eyes again. He tried to keep the question back again as he forced his smile to return.

"Hey, it's okay. You're my guest. You can do whatever you want."

A smile slowly spread on her face as she took a bite of her breakfast, making Luke's smile grow.

"You can even do me if you want," he joked.

He laughed when he looked up to see her coughing, almost choking before drinking some orange juice. She looked over at him after clearing her throat.

"Jerk." She said simply.

This caused Luke to laugh harder. He had missed these moments with her. He could tease and joke with her forever and would never grow tired of it.

"So, I was thinking, we could pick up some things for you, if you want," Luke said, through a mouthful of food.

When she didn't answer, he looked up and saw her staring at him.

"What?" he asked, after swallowing.

"First off, don't talk with your mouth full," she answered, pretending to wipe off food particles from her face. "Second, you don't have to," she said, playing with her food.

"Babe, I don't mind," Luke offered.

He watched a smile sneak up on her face again before she looked up at him.

"Okay, cowboy, if you want to waste money on me," she joked.

"I always do."

She let out a short laugh that made him grin. He had missed hearing her laugh in the house.

***

As they drove into town, Kate seemed to be more like herself before she left, singing her heart out with every song that came on the radio. Once in a while, Luke would join in, but most of the time he would just listen and enjoy.

They pulled up to the first store so she could get some clothes. He didn't mind her wearing his shirts as it reminded him of the time after making love, when she would parade around the house in one of his shirts. As he got out of the car, he quickly adjusted himself before opening the car door for Kate. She smiled at him as he hung his arm on the door with his thumb hitched on his belt. All he could do was stand there, smile, and stare at her.

"Well, am I allowed out of the car, or do I have stay in it?" she joked.

Luke shook his head before moving out of the way. Walking past him, he quickly shut the door and went to open the store's door. She laughed before flashing him a smile. Once again, he was stuck in her trance as he still couldn't believe she was here with him.

As they walked in, he felt eyes on them. Looking around, he saw some of the locals watching them and whispering to each other. He could imagine what they were whispering about. They probably couldn't believe Kate was here either.

He noticed Kate didn't pay attention to anything that was going on around them as she made a beeline to a rack and started to go through the clothes. Walking over, giving everyone a quick stare down to make them mind their own business, he laid his folded arms on the rack and rested his head on them, just watching as Kate was oblivious to everything. Once in a while, she would look up and smile at him. He could watch her all day.

Eventually, she moved onto the next rack and Luke followed, but before she could go through the clothing someone popped up in front of her. She fell back on Luke as he held her. Glaring at the woman, he wished these people would leave them alone.

"Oh, my God, Kate, is that you?" the woman exclaimed.

"Yeah," Kate said, unsure.

"Oh my, hasn't it been a long time," she said, before lightly slapping Kate's arm. "How have you been?"

Luke's eyes widened, hoping that this wouldn't be the place where Kate explained what had happened to her. He wanted to ask her in private, not in public.

"Well, I've been good, you know, Mrs. Robinson."

"Well, child, you must come to church this Sunday and sing," Mrs. Robinson insisted.

"Oh, I don't know..." Kate started.

"Nonsense, child, you must. It'll be great to hear you and Luke here sing, again."

"Well..." she looked back at Luke before addressing the woman. "Sounds good, we'll be there." She managed, with a fake smile.

"Oh, thank you." She turned to Luke. "Oh, Luke, are you doing one of your songs or something else?"

Luke's eyes got big. "Ahhh..." he started, before glancing in Kate's direction.

Mrs. Robinson got her attention back to her when she placed Kate's hand inside her own.

"Oh, child, you should hear Luke's songs.".

Luke tried to stop Mrs. Robinson from talking anymore, using a hand gesture for her to stop. Mrs. Robinson furrowed her brow.

"Luke, are you okay?" she asked.

He quickly whipped his hand behind his head as Kate squinted her eyes at him. He didn't need Kate to know what Mrs. Robinson was talking about as they were taking baby steps back into their relationship. Soon,

Kate's attention went back to Mrs. Robinson when she started to talk to her.

"Well, it was nice to see you, Kate, but I have to get going."

"Okay."

Turning to look at Luke with her arms crossed.

"What was that about?"

"No idea," Luke answered, shrugging his shoulders.

Luke crossed his arms to keep her from seeing them shake. She stared at him for a while until she eventually got bored and turned back around. Sighing a sigh of relief, he was glad she didn't dig further into it and continued to follow her around the store as she looked through the clothes. He could see her holding shirts up to herself and looking at the tag before placing them back on the rack. He started to wonder why she wasn't picking out any clothing. She seemed to like most of them, but her arms remained empty. He moved in front of her to stop her. She crashed into him with her hands on his chest. At first he saw fear in her eyes, but then they faded into the innocence that used to drive him crazy with lust.

"Don't you like any of those clothes?"

***

Kate looked at her hands as she felt the rumble from his chest before he spoke. Closing her eyes before speaking, she had to calm herself as all her old feelings for him were rekindling themselves. She could see the concern he had for her still there after all these years. She pretended to play with a fuzzy on his shirt, looking at it as if it were one of those weeds with prickles on them and it was hard to remove.

"Yeah," she said quietly.

"What?" he asked, leaning his head down.

"Yeah, I do," she answered with increased volume.

"Then why aren't you getting them?" he asked softly.

Looking back at the imaginary fuzzy. "They're too expensive," she said, fiddling her fingers.

"That's okay. You can get them if you want," he offered.

She sighed. "Let's just go to the Salvation Army shop... I don't need anything crazy expensive," she pleaded.

Luke chuckled before rolling his eyes. Pulling her hands away from his chest to have them encased in both of his, he brought them inches from his mouth as he looked at them before speaking.

"Kate, it's okay. You can get whatever you want."

"But, you don't have that kind of money," she said, confusion in her voice.

He smiled. "It's okay. I do," he said, before bringing her hands up to kiss her knuckles.

Her hands shook even with them encased in his. She didn't understand how he could afford such clothing. As she recalled, they lived on simple means, nothing crazy. They were doing simple gigs and side jobs to get through the bills. The only thing they had going was that the house was paid off before his parents passed away and left it to him. She wasn't sure what to do. It had been years since she had felt like this, and how he was treating her brought it all back. Swallowing hard, she decided she would just go with the way her heart was leading her. Looking at his face, she put on a smile, trying to distract him from the tears gathering on her lower eyelid.

"Thanks, Luke," she muttered.

He planted a soft kiss on her forehead, causing her to close her eyes, letting a tear fall, as her emotions whirled inside her like a tornado. She didn't know why she left him behind. He was the best thing to happen to her and she tossed him aside like a broken toaster. She didn't deserve him and she didn't deserve him being so acceptable to her. He should have been pissed for her leaving, but he was there with opened arms and offering so much to her. She always loved that southern hospitality. Smiling again, he pulled away as they locked eyes.

"You're welcome, babe," he said softly.

She flinched when his finger touched her cheek, but laughed to herself as she knew he would never hurt her. When she realized what he was doing, she watched him to see what he was going to say next, as he wiped the tear off her face. All he did was look at her before he gave her his sweet smile. All she could do was stand there and stare at him, still contemplating what an idiot she had been for leaving.

Chuckling, he turned her around and wrapped an arm around her shoulders as he led her to a rack of clothes.

"Now, come on, babe, let's get something for you."

Kate let him lead her as she intertwined her fingers with his on her shoulder. She couldn't help, but let out a giggle as well. It really did feel like old times.

***

Kate sat in the passenger seat, thinking about what she was feeling. Luke was outside the car, putting gas in the tank. After doing some shopping, she was surprised that he could afford so many things. She started to wonder if the price of cattle had gone up for him to be able to afford such things. Just as he always had, he would give the clerk crumpled up paper money. The clerk didn't seem to mind as she took it. Kate recalled all the times the clerks hated them as they were literally counting out change to buy something. When she got in the car, she saw the change jar that they used to carry around with them to help pay for something was still in the car. The only thing that didn't feel normal with Luke was when he was freaking over near the magazines. He quickly turned the ones in front around so only the backs were showing. She wasn't sure what the deal was, but ignored it as she spotted a candy bar. Without thinking, she grabbed it and placed it on the counter. She hadn't done anything like that for a long time, but she felt it was okay with Luke as he seemed to want her to have whatever she wanted.

***

Luke leaned up against the car as he waited for the gas tank to fill. Exhaling sharply, he recalled how Kate almost found out about his past secret life by the magazines that were on the rack. He had to quickly turned them around and blocked them before she saw them. Then some of the locals almost blew his cover when they started to talk to Kate. Good thing she was still distracted with her thoughts. Putting his hands in his jeans' pockets and crossing his legs, he started to bite his lower lip as he so wanted to ask her what had happened to her all those years she was gone, but his stomach would twist and turn and cause heartburn where he couldn't be brave enough to ask.

The click of the pump brought him back from his thoughts. He quickly pulled the hose out and placed it back on the station before getting into the car, not wanting any more time away from Kate. When he looked over, he noticed that she had been quiet and looking out the window a lot. Shaking her knee, she look at his hand first before looking at him.

"Are you okay?"

"Yeah."

"You sure?"

She looked at him with that small smile, and he knew there was something wrong. Kate only nodded her head to answer his question. He didn't want to let this go, but he knew she wasn't going to open up anytime soon. So, he started the car up and drove away from the gas station. As they drove, he kept his hand on her leg. Even though, he should feel happy, he still felt awful about how she was treated before. His mind just couldn't go back to their happy selves.

As he slowed down to an intersection and stopped, he drummed his thumb on the steering wheel after turning on his right turn signal. Checking to make sure there wasn't any traffic coming, he looked down all three roads. Without warning, he felt something on his crotch area before feeling a squeeze. Looking down, he saw Kate's hand squeezing him. Looking over, his mouth hanging open, he wasn't sure what was going on. Unbuckling herself, she slid closer to him so her mouth was inches away from his ear.

"Let's make it like old times," she whispered, seductively.

He just stared at her, not believing what he was hearing. As she leaned back and had the smirk on her face that she used to, he blinked a few times to get focus. Smiling big, he quickly changed the turn signal to the left. Peeling from the stop sign, he raced to their destination, engine roaring with its battle cry. She moved his hand from her leg and put it behind her as she leaned down and her hands messed with his belt and pants.

"What are you doing?" he asked, shock in his voice.

She looked up at him with a big smile on her face. He loved that she had that happiness sparkling in her eyes, but he still didn't know what was happening.

"Like I said, let's do it like old times… remember the game?" she teased.

Before he could answer, she had him in her mouth. He almost jumped out of the seat and ended up pressing harder on the gas, causing the car to shoot forward with a whine. Shifting back into the seat, he had forgotten about the game. Gripping the steering wheel until he became white knuckled, he knew what she was trying to do. He had to race back home without coming in her mouth or else he lost the challenge. Of course, if he was pulled over or got in trouble, she would still win.

"Oh, Jesus..." he choked out as she started working him hard.

Occasionally, he would look down to see her head bobbing up and down, but eventually he would have to focus on driving so he wouldn't release yet. Clenching his jaw, he could feel her getting him close, but then backing off. As he raced around, trying to get home, his body began to shake from the oral torture. He wanted to just let go, but he knew that would ruin her fun and he wanted her to enjoy it as much as possible. He tried humming with the radio to keep his mind off what was happening, but he involuntarily looked down and became harder in her mouth.

"Come on, come on," he whispered to himself.

"That's the goal," she said, before going back down on him.

A muffled whimper escaped his clenched jaw as she just made it worse. He still couldn't believe how long it was taking to get home as it wasn't that far from where they were. His body eventually started to involuntarily jerk toward her as if she needed help.

"Oh, please... please, please, please," he started to beg.

As he turned down onto a dirt driveway, he was glad to see the sight before him.

"Yes... yes, yes, yes," he chanted excitedly.

At that moment, he saw they were still too far for his victory. He hated that this driveway was so long when playing this game. His foot pressed harder on the gas as the car jerked around from all the bumps in the dirt road. It wasn't helping him, but her. He could feel he was so close to the edge. Finally, sliding into a spot next to the shed, the tires froze and slid on the dirt.

"Oh, thank God," he said in a husky voice, as he leaned his head back and his arms collapsed from his sides, panting.

Kate sat up and laughed at him. She wrapped her arms around him and leaned close to his ear.

"You finally won," she teased, with a laugh.

Before he could respond, she leaned in and kissed him hard on his lips. Pulling her on his lap, he held her tight against him, a small smile on the corner of his mouth, as he couldn't hide his happiness at having her here with him. His left hand went searching for the door lever so he could get her where he wanted her. As they got out of the car, she wrapped her legs around him, making their kissing more passionate as their tongues danced around each other's.

Lucky for him, her legs did a good job of keeping his jeans up so he wouldn't have to worry about tripping over them. Once he reached the wall of the structure, he pressed her against it so he could grind hard into her to show how much he wanted her like the old days. Leaving her lips, he trailed kisses along her jawline down to the nape of her neck. As she held onto him, he ripped open the front of her tank top as he wanted to taste all of her body as his taste buds had forgotten her. His hands found her perfect, rounded butt cheeks and squeezed them, causing her pelvis to push forward against him as she released a squeal. He stopped kissing her to look at her, inches from her face, as his eyes searched hers. It all seemed so long ago, but yet, here they are as if that much time hadn't passed. It was as if they just saw each other yesterday.

Slamming his lips back on hers before carrying her into the shed, he found an old tractor and gently slid her off him and onto her feet. Undoing her jeans, he gradually slid them down, still looking straight at her. As he came back up to her face, his fingers softly slid up her legs. He looked down after locking eyes with her for a second, a smile slowly forming on his face as he liked what he saw her wearing.

"Mmmm, white lace," he said, huskily.

"Only for you, cowboy," she said, seductively.

After removing the torn shirt, he saw she was wearing a white lace bra as well. He could feel his pants become tighter from the view. Slowly turning her around, he bend her over the hood of the tractor and leaned back to admire the view. Licking his lips, he fell to his knees and began to trail featherly kisses on her butt cheeks.

He gradually stood up and rubbed the palm of his hand in circles on one of her butt cheeks before spanking it. He smiled more when he heard her let out a moan. He did the same thing again and continued to listen to her. He was itching to be inside her, but at the same time he was enjoying this. Once both of her butt cheeks were nice and rosy pink, he slid his jeans down a little so he could free himself.

He gradually pushed himself into her, letting her clenched muscles get used to him, inch by inch. Once fully in, he paused and let her enjoy him. She started moving so he could slide in and out of her as he let out a chuckle before gripping her hips and thrusting into her hard and fast. As much as he enjoyed staring at her rosy, pink ass, he decided he didn't want her like this.

"This won't do," he said, quietly.

He heard her let out a whimper when he pulled out, but once he had her on her back, she smiled up at him with a haze in her eyes.

"I need to have you this way," he said, huskily, putting his arms under her legs so they were pressed against her body.

He began thrusting into her again, watching her at first as she enjoyed him. Then pressed his face into the nape of her neck, muffling his grunts. As he buried himself farther into her, he felt so lost into her, as her moans fell into his ears. He never imagined they would be back to this, although he always hoped that she would return to him. Her fingernails dug deep into his shoulder blades, causing him to jerk harder into her. Fisting her hips and clenching his jaw, he tried to hold back, but when she licked his ear and bit down on his earlobe it caused him to go over the edge of ecstasy. As he bucked the last of his release, her fingernails scratched down his back as she released around him.

As he enjoyed the feeling, he started to feel dizzy and rested his head against her shoulder, closing his eyes to will it away. Feeling something softly touching his face, he could hear her breathing had changed and felt eyes on him.

"Are you okay?"

"Yeah… just a little winded," he said, with a chuckle.

She laughed. "I would say that was some ride," she joked.

Once he felt that his head wasn't spinning too much, he picked her up and moved her to some hay that was piled on the ground. Before laying her down, he threw a blanket over the top of it so the straw wouldn't be poking them. He gradually laid them down on the ground before turning on his side. Putting a hand to his forehead, he could hear his heartbeat pounding as the dizziness came back. He could feel her hand on his face again as he smiled to show her he was okay. Removing his hand, he looked at her as she still had the haze in her eyes from her orgasm. Stroking her face softly, he really missed her. As his heart started to slow down, he knew she was his calming factor as she always had a peaceful look about her. Leaning down, he trailed kisses on her collarbone.

"Stay with me," he begged, softly.

He didn't realize that he had said it as it was floating around in his mind. Now, all he could do was stare at her. He could see the confusion in her eyes at first and then they lit up when a smile appeared on her face.

"Yes," she whispered.

His heart started to pound harder again and he felt his head spinning, but he didn't care. He had received the greatest news in the world. He leaned down and gently kissed her lips before she wrapped her arms around him, pulling him on top of her. He began to rock into her as he felt alive again as it had been a long time since he had.

CHAPTER THREE

Rolling onto her side, Kate slowly opened her eyes. It took her a moment to realize where she was as she stared at the acoustic guitar leaning against a wooden chair. Memories of yesterday flashed through her mind as she quickly sat up, covering herself up with the blanket as she realized she was still naked. Closing her eyes once her hand touched her forehead, she started to regret what she did. Eventually, she stood and let her fingers strum the strings on the guitar as a memory of him playing it and singing to her to help her sleep came back to her. She reached the mirror and brushed away some loose strands from her face. Leaning on the dresser on one hand, she stared at herself.

"What are you doing, Kate?" she asked herself.

Looking around, she found some clothing, and quickly dressed before heading downstairs. She didn't want to continue walking around like an invitation to more sex.

"Luke?" she called out, walking down the stairs.

She continued to look for him as she didn't see him in the living room.

"Luke?" she called out again, entering the kitchen.

Looking across, she spotted her name on a folded piece of paper on the fridge. Walking over to it, she pulled it from the fridge, letting the magnet hit the floor. Opening it up, she read:

Dear Kate,

It's going to get really hot out and I ask that you stay inside today so you won't get heatstroke. I ran to the store for food as we didn't get a chance to do that yesterday ;)

Love ya,

Luke

Kate kept rereading the note, especially the last sentence, as her stomach became a big knot. She still couldn't believe what she did yesterday. Why did she think it was like the old days when in reality she was just staying here until the bus came back? Letting the note drop as she was done reading it, she decided she needed to go for a walk to clear her head. If she spent one more moment in the house, she might not want to leave.

As she stepped outside, she looked up at the sun that was barely up. Even though it wasn't cold out, she felt a chill and closed her eyes to let the sun warm her up. Opening her eyes, she started to walk. She had no clue where she was going, but she needed to keep moving. Looking around, she noticed that the old place was still the same as she remembered. Once she was past the farmland, walked on the dirt road that led to another property. Wrapping her arms around her, she stared at the ground as she went through all the thoughts in her head. She was both confused and scared, and didn't know how to salvage the situation. She didn't want to break Luke's heart again, but she knew she was damaged goods and needed to get away from it all.

As she continued to walk, her mind started to get fuzzy. Shaking her head, she didn't know what was happening until her vision became tunneled. Before she could do anything, she collapsed. Rolling onto her back, she stared up at the sky. With her shaky arm, she tried to shield her eyes from the sun, but soon it fell next to her and her eyes closed.

***

Letting out a groan, she felt something cool and wet on her stomach. Occasionally, she could feel the same on her face. As she licked her lips, she could feel that they were cracked and chapped. As a wet, cool cloth lay on her forehead, she tried to sit up, but felt a couple of hands on her, trying to lay her down.

"Easy, Kate," Luke said softly.

"What happened?" she questioned with a groan.

"You got some heatstroke," he answered.

Groaning again, she couldn't believe she was so stupid for going outside. She should have known better. She paused as she realized her old self would have known better, not the new city girl that she had grown to be.

"Here, drink some water."

His hand slid behind her to help her sit up. As she sat up, she didn't go toward the direction of the glass but to his lips. She continued to kiss him as she started to feel relaxed against him, then a thought popped in her head, causing her to whip away from him.

"I'm sorry…that was a mistake."

"A mistake?"

She could hear the pain in his voice when he asked. Closing her eyes, she couldn't bear to do this now with him as tears started to run down her face. She tried hiding them by covering her face with both hands, but it was too late as he had her wrapped in his arms and on his lap in seconds, rocking her.

"What's wrong, babe?" he asked with concern.

This caused her to cry harder and her sobbing kept her vocal cords too busy to answer him. She couldn't believe how hard she had fallen for him again and now she was going to rip his heart out again. She tried to get away from him, but she didn't struggle hard enough against him. All she could was let him hush and rock her.

"Please, Kate, tell me what's wrong?" he whispered into her ear.

"I'm a horrible person," she finally choked out.

"What...who would think that?"

"Everyone."

"Kate, that's crazy... you're not a horrible person."

"Yes, I am," she said sternly, removing her hands from her face.

"Why do you think that?" he questioned, furrowing his brow.

"Because I am."

"That's not a good reason."

"It is," she said, looking away from him.

***

Luke has no idea what Kate was going through. He had never seen her like this before and didn't know where it was coming from. He didn't really like this Kate. He wanted the old Kate that was happy and carefree. As he held her close, he didn't like how much she wasn't herself, especially the weight loss. He needed to find a way to help her heal from something that had damaged and destroyed her. Swallowing hard, he needed to know what he was up against.

"So, what happened to you?" he asked, his voice shaking.

Even though his heart was pounding in his ears, he heard as she stopped breathing and froze in his arms. He was worried this might happen, but for her to heal, he needed her to tell him what happened to make her a shadow of her former self.

"What?" she asked, in a quivering voice.

"Babe, I need to know what happened to you," he begged her.

Before he knew it, she stood and turned to look at him. He was actually terrified when he saw her face was twisted in hatred and anger.

"The hell you do!" she screamed.

"Babe, I..." he started, reaching out to her.

Slapping his hand away. "Fuck you, Luke!" she yelled.

He was caught off guard as he didn't expect this. She had always shared everything with him and he had never seen her hide something.

"You need to mind your own damn business and leave my life alone!" she yelled.

He watched as she stomped away and up the stairs in record timing, startled when she slammed the door. All he could do was stare up at the stairs, hoping that it was all a joke and she was going to come back down and be her old self. After what seemed like an eternity, he realized she wasn't going to come back down and it wasn't a joke. Dropping his head and closing his eyes, he realized he had really messed up this time. He gradually stood, even though the dizziness was back ten-fold, he was determined to make things right.

Taking his time up the stairs, he stood before the bedroom door. He stared at it for a long time before moving over to it cautiously. Exhaling sharply, he hoped this would work. Knocking, he waited for some type of response. Nothing happened, so he knocked again.

"Kate...Babe?"

Still no response. Sighing, he realized that he wouldn't be able to apologize tonight. Walking away, he went into the bathroom and slowly shut the door. Leaning over the sink, closing his eyes, he tried to calm his heart so the dizziness would go away.

"What have I done?" he asked himself quietly

***

Kate had kept the cries silent as she didn't need Luke kicking down the door. Of course, as she leaned against it on the floor, she imagined she would get hurt in the process. Closing her eyes as she let out a shaky breath, she could feel the past injuries she had received aching. She hated feeling like this, but she couldn't face her past now. Her heart wanted to tell Luke everything, but her mind wanted to shield him from it. Covering her face again, she didn't know what to do. She needed to get out of here before it was too late and she couldn't leave.

"What am I doing?" she whispered to herself.

33

***

Kate couldn't sleep much during the night, not because of all the thoughts whirling around her head, but Luke was outside the door playing the guitar. She knew he meant well as he tried to help her sleep with the soothing music. She didn't know why he just didn't come in as she hadn't locked the door, but at the same time was glad that he didn't as she could bear to look at him for all the hurt she had caused him. Tears welled up in her eyes again as she continued to lay there in bed. She just didn't have the strength to get up. She jumped and cried more when she heard the back screen door slam shut. She knew he must be off to do some farming. Even though, in the back of her mind, she thought this would be the perfect time to leave, her body didn't move at all as it was weighed down by her heart.

Eventually, she got up and dressed. Her feet started to lead her somewhere as she went down the stairs and slid on her shoes. Before she knew it, she was out the back screen door and continued to walk. Her mind knew she should have gone out the front door, but her heart wanted to go this way.

As she got closer to her destination, she could hear the tractor. Eventually, she saw it ride slowly past as it plowed the earth. Sitting on top, controlling it, was Luke wearing a cowboy hat to help protect him from the sun and had his shirt off. As she kept moving toward him, he started to notice her there. He stopped the machine and had a big grin on his face.

"Hey, there, Daisy Duke," he called out.

Kate stopped and looked down. She didn't realize the way was she was dressed. Rolling her eyes, she couldn't believe she was wearing such a get up as she wouldn't have dressed like this in her old life. The city life had made it difficult to be her old self.

"Sorry, I don't know what I was thinking!" she shouted.

"Hey, I'm not going to complain with those short shorts," he teased.

Rolling her eyes again and laughing, she walked closer to him more so she could stand right next to the big tractor. She shielded her eyes as she looked up at him.

"Having fun plowing?"

She watched as a bigger grin appeared on his face.

"I could think of better ways of using my time," he joked.

"Look... about last night," she started.

"Hey, why don't you come on up here and sit on my lap and see what pops up," he teased, patting his lap.

Kate rolled her eyes. "You're such a perv," she said with a laugh.

"Come on...for ol' time's sake?" he asked.

"Fine, but don't think we're not going to talk about last night," she said, sternly.

"Hey, we can talk whatever you want, babe."

She slowly made her way on the tractor with him as he held out his hand to help pull her up. She sat on his right leg as his right arm wrap around her waist to make sure she was secure and safely on it. He started the tractor and it slowly started to move.

"So, about last night..." she started again.

"You know what, I want to talk about something else."

Squinting her eyes at him. "I thought you said we can talk about whatever I wanted?" she questioned.

"I know... I lied. Sorry, babe, but seeing you with those short shorts makes me want to have some fun like we used to," he teased.

Rolling her eyes at him. "Whatever," she said.

His hand slithered down until it was on the inside of her thigh. "Oh, come on, you don't miss this?" he asked, placing a soft kiss on her cheek.

"No," she answered, after pushing his hand away and crossing her arms.

"Are you sure?" he asked, sliding his hand back to the inside of her thigh.

***

Luke smiled when he could see her slowly giving in as her tense face loosened. Remembering all the times they messed around on the tractor made him harden more. He took the chance and slowly slid his fingers under the shorts to feel the cotton panties she was wearing.

"Hmm, no lace today?" he asked.

"Nope," she answered sternly.

Sliding his fingers farther in, his smile grew when he felt something.

"You know, your face is saying no, but your body is betraying you by saying yes," he teased.

"I don't know what you're talking about," she said quickly.

"You're wet," he said, huskily, close to her ear.

As his fingers moved over her panties, he heard the air catching in her throat. He knew she was enjoying this even though she was trying to act as if she wasn't. He found the edge of the cotton barrier and slid his fingers in and felt her body responding to his touch.

Watching as her eyes slowly closed and her body relaxed against his, her arm slithered up until her hand rested on the back of his head. Each time his fingers touched somewhere special, she would fist some of his hair, letting out small whimpers.

As his two of his fingers slid in, she let out a louder moan. Smiling more, he liked making her dance with them. Listening to her body, he knew she was getting close. Planting a soft kiss on her neck after licking up the sweat from it. He pressed his forehead next to her face.

"That's it, babe... come on my fingers," he whispered, breathily.

After saying those words, she convulsed on him, as he tried his best to keep her on his lap. Licking up her neck again, he had his mouth near her ear again.

"Babe, that was so hot," he whispered.

"Yes," she whimpered, as she calmed down, panting.

Luke could feel himself pressed hard against his jeans. As she kept rubbing herself against him, he knew what he needed.

"I so need you, babe," he said through clenched jaw.

Before she could protest, he stopped the tractor and had her in his arms as he jumped off the farm equipment. She was about to say something, but he slammed his lips on hers to keep her quiet. He didn't want to hear any objections from her, but only those sweet, pleasure sounds when he made her come again.

Walking into a wooded area, he found the perfect place, before laying down with her. As he grind into her, she pushed him away. He was going to object as he knew they both wanted it, but to his surprise, she pulled down her shorts and panties before he went back between her legs. Untying her flannel shirt where she had it tied up, he pushed it opened to reveal a simple cotton bra. He didn't care what she was wearing underneath just as long as he could get under it and feel her body.

His lips were back on hers after undoing his jeans and belt. Rocking into her, he felt her feet on the waistline of his jeans and pushed them down farther before hooking her ankles behind him. This caused him to push harder into her from the simple rocking. As his lips traveled everywhere that skin was showing, he couldn't believe this was all happening. He had missed making love to her outside as they used to.

"Oh, Luke…" she whispered.

Chills ran across his skin when she said his name. It had been so long since he heard her say it like that. He wanted to stay like this forever, but he knew he wouldn't last long if she kept being so damn sexy.

"Oh, God, Luke… right there," she moaned.

His grunts went with the rhythm he found that she liked. As he continued to nibble and lick her neck, he listened to the pleasure sounds coming out of her mouth.

"Oh, Luke, I'm so close… please keep going," she begged.

"Christ, you're so sexy when you talk like that," he said, huskily.

He licked up her neck. "Oh God, you taste so fucking awesome, too," he groaned.

Pulling his face away from the nape of her neck, she looked into his eyes. "Shut up and fuck me," she ordered.

"Yes, babe."

As he passionately kissed her, he thrust harder and deeper into her. Before he knew it, she convulsed under him before clenching tightly around him. The one last push caused him to teeter over the edge and he clenched his jaw as the air rushed through his teeth in a hissing sound. Pulling her tighter against him, they released together. Once the effects of their orgasms went away, his body and breathing were shaky. Forcing himself to hold himself up, he stared into Kate's hazed over eyes. Leaning down, he gently kissed her lips as his heart pounded in his chest. It had been forever since he felt such a thrill as the dizziness swarmed his mind. He leaned his forehead against hers, exhaling sharply. He felt her hand as he slowly moved his face to make if feel as if she was stroking it.

"Are you okay?" she asked, quietly.

A big smile spread across his face. "Beyond the stars better," he joked, with a chuckle.

Opening his eyes, he could see a smile appearing on her face. He still couldn't believe she was right back where she belonged... with him.

CHAPTER FOUR

Luke had Kate on her back as they lay on the couch together, in only their undergarments. They were making out after pretty much not doing much work around the farm. He pulled away to brush some hair back from her face.

"I love you," he whispered.

"I love you, too."

His smile stretched across his face as he felt the happiness in his heart. Returning to her lips, he was about to enter her, but then a sound of a door opening caught his attention.

"Oh, Luke..." A woman walked in before her eyes landed on Luke's backside. "Oh, my God!" she yelled.

Luke jumped up, trying to put his need back inside his boxers. Kate handed him his cowboy hat, and he covered himself with it as he was still standing at attention in his boxers. He couldn't believe of all the times, this had to happen.

"What the hell, Luke! Ever heard of being covered up?" she screamed.

"Ever heard of knocking?" he yelled back.

"Don't you use that tone on me, mister," she said, sternly.

"Don't you see I have a guest here?"

"Yeah, I do, and I don't appreciate it." She retorted, pointing a finger at him. "You shouldn't be doing this, because you're in love with Kate…"

She looked at Kate before looking back at Luke, did double-take and stared at Kate.

"Kate?" she questioned, confusion in her voice.

"Hi, CindyLou," Kate said nonchalantly, with a hand up to wave.

CindyLou stood there frozen before her face changed to pure excitement.

"Oh my God! Kate!" she screamed, with her arms wide open.

She ran right over and hugged Kate tightly, ignoring the fact she was only in her bra and panties.

"Um, you mind telling me what you're doing here?" Luke asked.

CindyLou let go of Kate and stood next to Luke, reached out, and pinched his cheek.

"I'm here to check on my little baby brother," she baby talked.

Swatting her hand away. "I'm fine," he answered quickly.

"Well, I see you are now," she said with a big smile. "I'm so glad I came in when I did or else I would have been scarred for life," she joked.

Rolling his eyes. "You're such a creep," he said.

"No, I didn't want to see anything, especially my baby brother standing here like a stripper… Now, for the love of God, get dressed," she ordered, flicking the cowboy hat still covering him.

He huffed. "Fine," he said, before stomping his foot.

CindyLou turned to look at Kate before sitting down next to her.

"So, how's my favorite sister-in-law?" she asked, excitement on her face.

"Um… one, Luke and I aren't married," Kate began to answer.

"Close enough, let's not get technical," CindyLou said, waving it away.

40

"Two, if we were, I would be your only sister-in-law, so you wouldn't have many choices," Kate finished.

"Oh stop, girl… let's not get so deep into it. Tell me, when did you get in?" CindyLou pushed.

Kate looked over at Luke who had been watching the whole time he was putting his jeans back on. Luke shook his head as he walked over to his sister, grabbing her by her arm to lead her toward the door.

"Time to go, CindyLou," he ordered.

She looked at him shocked. "No way, I just got here," she protested.

He opened the door and pushed her out. "Goodbye, Sis."

Pushing the door open. "I can't leave, there's so much we have to catch up on, like the fact about your rise to…" she struggled to say.

Luke's eyes went wide as he shoved the door closed, but she pushed it open enough to squeeze her face in.

"Oh, and the part about your…" she started.

"Goodbye, CindyLou," he said sternly, before shutting the door all the way.

He quickly locked it and spun around to press his back to it, and closed his eyes. He knew it was locked, but he wanted to make sure there was no way for her to get in. Exhaling, he could feel his heart pounding against his chest again as the dizziness swarmed again. He really wished people would just leave them alone. Opening his eyes slowly, he saw Kate walking toward him slowly with one of his flannel shirts on with the front opened. He tried to calm himself as she walked so damn sexy toward him. Once, she was standing in front of him, he felt as if all the air rushed out of him.

"Wow, she hasn't changed," Kate joked.

"Yeah," he said, once he was able to breathe again.

Placing her hands on his chest, she looked at them before looking at him.

"So, what now, cowboy?" she questioned, seductively.

He smiled before stroking her face. "Us," he answered quietly, before leaning in to kiss her.

He so wanted to enjoy these moments with Kate, but there was the nagging thought in the back of his mind that kept bothering him. He couldn't shake it, but didn't want to ruin his time with Kate so he ignored it.

It's about us now…

***

Kate threw the dart and hit the right spot. She threw up her arms and yelled out a victory sound as Luke pulled her tighter against him with a big smile on his face. He turned her face so he could kiss her again between playing darts. Pulling away, he flicked his cowboy hat she's wearing.

"You look so hot in that," he flirted.

"And you look hot on me," she flirted back.

"Oh really," he said, pulling her closer to where their noses were touching.

CindyLou walked up with two beer bottles, rolling her eyes. "Oh, God, I believe I'm getting diabetes from all this sweetness," she groaned.

Kate turned to her. "Well, get a blood glucose meter to make sure you don't overdose on it," Kate joked.

Rolling her eyes. "Oh, Kate, oh how I missed you," CindyLou joked.

"I know you did."

"Well, sir and madam, here are your adult beverages."

"Thanks, Sis," Luke said, his arm wrapped around Kate.

"You're very welcome Baby Brother, I didn't want you to get carded," CindyLou teased.

"Oh, for the love of God, I'm not a baby," Luke said, shaking his head.

She leaned forward and pinched his cheek. "You will always be my baby brother," CindyLou teased.

Luke pulled away from CindyLou as Kate held up her hands.

"Excuse me, I hate to ruin this family time, but this girl needs to use the bathroom," she said with a smile.

"Don't be too long," Luke called after her.

Turning her head to look back at him. "I won't," she teased.

Luke couldn't remove his eyes from Kate, even after she disappeared into the crowd at the bar. The only thing that caught his attention was the feeling of someone staring at him. Looking over at his sister, he could see her giving him the 'Mom look'.

"What?" he asked, before taking a drink from the beer bottle.

"What do you mean, what? Have you told her yet?" CindyLou probed.

"Not yet," he answered, looking away from her.

"Luke!"

Standing up from the bar stool. "Why ruin the good times, C?" He looked over where Kate disappeared into the crowd before looking back at CindyLou. "Just mind your own," he grated.

"Luke, it's not fair to her," she said, with concern in her voice.

"Don't worry about it, C."

Grabbing his arm before he walked away. "Please, Luke... Don't do this to her," she begged.

Luke pulled his arm out of her grip. "C, I'm not doing any harm," he reassured her.

"You are, if you don't tell her."

He looked down at the ground before looking her in the face again, pointing at her.

"Look, when you have a relationship that works, then you can counsel me on relationships. Until then, mind your own," he said angrily.

CindyLou stared at him wide-eyed.

"Now, excuse me, I have the love of my life to be with," he said, before pushing past her, bumping into her shoulder.

"Well, alrighty then," she whispered to herself, before taking a big swig of her drink.

Shaking her head, she lets out a hoot before looking around.

"Time to find mister right," she said, before walking away.

***

As usual, there was a long line for the ladies room, so, like the old days, Kate used the men's room. She didn't care as she knew most of these people and they weren't surprised by it. As she started to walk back to where she left Luke and CindyLou, she bumped into someone and found herself staring at a familiar face, but couldn't believe how clean cut it was.

"Johnboy?" she questioned.

"Kate?"

"Oh, my God, Johnboy how have you been?" she asked.

"Oh, great, but now I'm a lawyer so I don't go by Johnboy anymore," he answered.

"Oh, I'm sorry."

"Nah, it's okay. You can still call me Johnboy as well as Luke."

"So, a lawyer huh?"

"Yeah, I know, a big surprise for everyone, even my 'rents."

"Yeah…" she said, still shocked.

"So, Kate… How have you been?"

***

Luke caught Johnboy asking the same question that everyone had asked already, wondering if Kate was going to break down and tell the truth.

"Oh, fine. You know," she said, simply.

Luke clenched his jaw as he wished she would just tell someone what had happened to her so he could do something about it.

"So, I'm guessing you and Luke are back together?" Johnboy asked.

"How do you know?"

Pointing at the flannel shirt she was wearing. "I'd recognize that shirt anywhere," he laughed.

Pulling on the shirt, she joked, "Oh, yeah... Sorry, I thought the CindyLou paper was already announcing it."

"So, have you heard about Luke?" he asked.

"What about him?" she questioned, tilting her head to the side.

"Well, after you left..." Johnboy started.

Luke's eyes widened and he rushed in to stop him from telling Kate his secrets.

"Hey, there you are," Luke said, with his back toward Johnboy.

"Hey, Luke... sorry I was talking to Johnboy here," she said, before looking over Luke's shoulder at Johnboy.

Luke slowly turned his head around and smiled at Johnboy. "Hey, man, what's been happening?" he asked.

"Oh nothing much besides lawyer stuff," he answered, before looking over at Kate. "So, what I was saying..." he started.

Luke turned around and put his hand out to shake Johnboy's hand.

"Hey, man, sorry gotta go," he quickly said.

"Um, okay," Johnboy said, with confusion in his voice.

"And we don't want to bore Kate with those stories," he stated, squeezing Johnboy's hand.

Johnboy looked at their hands before looking up at Luke with a smile.

"Gotcha," he said, quickly.

"Good," Luke said, before letting go of Johnboy's hand.

"Nice seeing you again, Kate. We'll catch up another time," Johnboy said, before leaving.

Luke turned around and could see that Kate had furrowed her brow, tilting her head and crossing her arms.

"What was that about?" she asked.

"No idea," he answered, shrugging his shoulders.

She continued to stare at him. He could tell she didn't believe him, but he didn't want to talk about things right now, just as she didn't want to talk about what had happened to her.

"So, hey, let's go somewhere a bit more private," he suggested.

She continued to stare at him until he finally saw that she wasn't interested in what almost happened.

"Okay."

"Awesome," he said, quickly, as he led her out of the bar with his hand on her back.

***

Luke and Kate almost fell when he opened the door. Luckily, he caught them as they continued to make out. On their way home she made it difficult for him to focus on driving as she was being as sexy as hell. She was groping him and eventually slid her hand in his jeans and stroked him. She wanted to keep making out, but he had to keep an eye on the road so they wouldn't crash. He was half-tempted to pull off to the side and take care of her needs before going home, but he knew they would be there the whole night.

Pressing her against the wall, he began to rock against her as all he wanted to do was rip her clothes off and just bury himself in her. Picking her up with his hands fisting her ass, she wrapped her legs above his hips as he let out a groan. She skimmed over his steel-hard need that was pressing against his jeans, wanting to be freed to feel such pleasures from her. He was about to take her upstairs to give her a full night of ecstasy to make up for lost time, but she pulled away.

"Before we go have fun, I could use a drink," she requested.

He smiled before kissing her again as they made their way to the kitchen. He placed her on top of the counter as he continued making out with her and rocking into her. He really didn't want to move from his spot as their tongues twirled around each other, causing chills to run along his skin.

This was amazing until he started to feel it. It first started out with his heart palpating like crazy and then the dizziness spinning in his head like a tornado. His legs started to wobble and become numb. Before he could do anything, he reached out to try to hold onto the counter, but his blurred vision caused him to miss grabbing it as he went down. Soon, the blurred vision turned to tunnel vision, until all he could see was darkness. He felt his hand on his forehead and Kate's hands on him. He didn't know if he was convulsing or if it was her shaking him as she yelled something that was muffled to him. Before he knew it, he passed out.

***

Luke woke up to a bright, shining light in his eye. Swatting it away, his vision cleared and he spotted a couple of EMTs crouched down next to him on either side. He had no idea what they were doing here until he tried springing up. He didn't get far as the dizziness caused him to lay back down with his hand on his forehead again.

"Whoa, sir, you need to relax," one EMT stated.

"No, I need to find Kate," he said, groggily.

"It's okay, she's in the next room… you gave her a scare," the other EMT said.

As Luke lay there, he couldn't believe it had happened in front of her. He thought he had more time, but now it seemed like it shortened.

"What a fucking idiot," he whispered to himself.

***

Kate just stared into the kitchen. She heard that Luke was awake, but the sheriff wouldn't let her go to him. All she could see were his boots as they moved. She could have guessed he tried getting up.

Looking back at the sheriff, she asked, "I'm sorry, did you need anything else from me?"

"No, ma'am."

"Then can I go to him?" she begged, with a little cry in her voice.

"Once the EMTs were done."

Kate kept looking back at the kitchen, hoping everything was okay. Eventually, the EMTs came out as she watched them walk up to her.

"Now, ma'am, he just needs to rest for a while," one EMT said.

"What happened?"

"Sorry, that's private," the EMT sighed.

"Oh okay," Kate said, quietly.

They left her in the living as she wrapped her arms around herself, suddenly feeling the chill. Her mind tried to figure out what happened to Luke as she stared at the ground.

***

As Luke leaned up against the wall after leaving the kitchen, he could see the worried expression on Kate's face. He had been afraid this might happen.

"Luke," she called out.

He huffed when she ran to him and crashed into him to wrap her arms around him. Once out of being startled, he wrapped his arms around her as well. He could feel her shaking, and then the sound of crying, as he felt moisture against his shirt. Screwing his eyes shut, he hated that she was worried about him.

"I'm sorry, Kate," he whispered.

She pulled away from him, placing a hand on his face.

"Are you okay?"

Staring at her tear-stained face, it was killing him inside as his heart dropped and his stomach twisted.

"Kate... I have to," he started.

"Yes, Luke," she said, looking at him with pleading in her eyes.

"I'm… I have…" he stuttered.

"What is it?"

Exhaling sharply. "I'm just a little dehydrated," he lied.

Kate squinted her eyes. He could tell she wasn't positive about his statement.

"So, I'll just need to rest and hydrate," Luke continued.

"Oh, okay, let's get you to bed," she offered.

Luke rolled his eyes at himself as he wished he hadn't lied to her, but he couldn't bring himself to tell her the truth. He didn't know why, but in the back of his mind, he didn't think she would want to be with him if she found out. He wanted… no, he needed her by his side. It was the wish he had been hoping would come true for the longest time, and he didn't want to jinx it now.

***

As Luke lay on his side, he pretended to be asleep as he listened to Kate strumming the strings on his guitar. She started out humming, and then it turned into words that he could barely hear. He really didn't know how to face her as he saw how worried she was last night. He started to think that maybe he should tell her the truth and let her leave before he caused anymore hurt.

Without warning, a hard cough escaped him. He froze, hoping that she hadn't noticed, but she stopped singing and he heard her set down his guitar. Rolling over on his back, he watched as she crawled across the bed toward him. He became speechless again as the sunlight flooded in enough to cause such a shine around her. She looked like an angel descending from heaven toward him in only a shirt and panties. Cupping his face made him come back to reality.

"Are you okay? Do you need anything," she asked softly.

"You."

He watched a smile form on her face. He was glad she wasn't too upset from last night. Before he knew it, her hand slid under the blanket as she rubbed the outside of his boxers. Swallowing hard, he could feel himself hardening more on top of the morning wood. Slowly, her hand slid under the cotton material and was stroking him. Closing his eyes, he let out a shaky breath.

"So, you just want little ol' me?" she teased.

Opening his eyes, he looked at her before lifting his hand and used the back of his index finger to rub her hardened nipple through her shirt.

"Oh, yeah, you're all I need, but there's just one problem," he flirted.

"And what's that?" she questioned, seductively.

"How can I just have you with this get up on?" he said playfully, with a pout.

He watched as she smiled before sitting up and removing the shirt and panties. He rested his arm behind his head as he watched as she started to fondle her breast and rub herself down there.

"You like what you see, cowboy?" she asked, with a tease.

"Yes, I do," he answered, in a husky tone.

"Then enjoy this," she said, before moving.

Before he knew it, she moved the blanket barrier that was between them and slowly sat astride him but backwards. Watching her every move, he inhaled quickly when she stroked him a few times with the hand between her legs before pushing him inside her. Once all the way inside, she moved her hand and leaned forward on both hands. Licking his lips, he hardened more inside her as she moved up and down on him. She was right, he was enjoying this as her ass was like a taunt to him.

Using his other hand, he slowly rubbed in circles on her one butt cheek before slapping it. He did the same with the other and kept going back and forth, which caused her to moan louder each time he did it. As he continued, he started to thrust up into her, but she stopped and looked over her shoulder.

"No, you need to rest," she ordered, with a tease.

He chuckled. "Okay, nurse, you know what's best," he flirted.

She started to ride him again as he enjoyed the position she was in, called the backwards cowgirl, as her ass kept flaunting around.

"Oh, God, I can't take much more of this," he said, through his teeth.

He got his arms under her legs and pulled her up and toward him. Covering his face with her as he began to eat her out. He listened as she whimpered and tried to pull away.

"Hell no, you're all mine," he said, pulling her back where he could taste her.

"Oh, Luke… let me do it all," she said, between whimpers.

Pulling away. "Oh, babe, you can, but right now, give me that fucking awesome head you like to give," he requested.

Letting out a long groan as she slid him slowly into her warm, wet mouth. He let her work him before he went back to his treat. Occasionally, he would pull away and slap her ass.

"Oh, babe, you're so fucking hot," he croaked.

He started to rock his hips toward her as her muffled moans vibrated against him. She even pulled him in all the way for him to feel that warmth snuggling of the back of her throat. Closing his eyes, he kept up with her pace as he wanted them to both let go at the same time. As he flicked his tongue against her clit, he felt the warmth disappeared off his need as she started to moan louder. He stopped.

"Hey, babe, don't you quit on me yet. I need you to fucking suck me dry," he ordered, huskily.

Within seconds, she was sucking and working him hard and fast. He smiled big before returning to her as he knew she was getting close. He could feel her muscles clenched around his fingers he snuck in between eating her out and bobbing his tongue in and out. As she pulsated against his mouth, he bucked a few times inside, touching the back of her throat. He let out a long muffled groan when he felt her doing what he asked her to do. She was sucking him dry so there weren't any of his seeds left.

Eventually, his body collapsed when he felt such pure exhaustion as his body vibrated with the release. He looked over when she curled up against him, smiling at him. He smiled back before cupping her face to kiss her gently.

Pulling away, he gently stroked her face with his knuckles.

"Oh, my God, babe, that was fucking amazing," he whispered.

"Mmm, yes it was."

"You're my fucking sexy vixen." His hand fisted her butt cheek. "And that fucking sexy ass of yours... I love making it a rosy pink," he supplied.

She giggled. "Mmm, I love you fucking me and feeling you inside me," she said seductively.

"Oh, babe, keep talking to me like that and I don't think I keep myself from doing so."

"Maybe, I don't want you to stop."

"Is that what you really want?" Arching his eyebrow.

"Fuck yeah... I want you to keep fucking me until I fall sleep with you still inside me."

Before the possibility of rethinking it, Luke was already on top and entering her hard and fast. He listened to her scream and holler in ecstasy as he pounded away. She gripped the headboard hard until her knuckles went white. He could tell she was trying to keep her release back, but he was going to make sure that she went over the edge many times to where she couldn't walk straight anymore.

"Is this how you want it?"

"Yes, Luke... give me all of it."

"All! You're going to get it all. I'll make sure of that."

"Oh, Luke, fuck me hard."

He smiled, loving how things were like the old times. As he continued to pound away, he watched her amazing tits bounce around to the rhythm of his thrusting into her.

His heart felt different as he gazed upon her. It was still hard to believe she was right here with him like the old days. He pressed his face into the nape of her neck, grunting away, making sure his heart wouldn't quit on him as he made love to his only love. Tightening his hold on her, a thought went through his mind.

I will never let her go... ever again...

CHAPTER FIVE

Luke stretched before rolling onto his side and wrapping his arm around his sexy beauty who was sleeping next to him. They spent most of the day yesterday fucking that eventually she was the first to wither and he did what she asked. She fell asleep with him still inside her. He couldn't stop watching his sleeping beauty sleep as she was so amazing.

He had been thinking all night as he kept trying to put away some of the thoughts he didn't want in his head as he was with his love. Eventually, an idea popped in his head and he couldn't wait for Kate to wake up so she could share in his plan.

He watched as a pair of light hazel eyes fluttered open. She slowly rolled onto her side to nuzzle against him.

"Mmm, morning," she said, satisfied.

"Morning, babe," he replied, before brushing a kiss in her hair.

"That was incredible last night," she moaned.

"Yeah, it was," he said, happily.

His smile slowly disappeared because he wasn't sure how he would say this to her as she seemed so cozy next to him. Brushing his fingers through her soft, feathery hair, he bit his lower lip as he thought of a way. Eventually, exhaling slowly, he decided to go ahead with it.

"I want a child with you," he said, slowly.

She looked at him with her brow furrowing. "What?" she asked, with confusion in her voice.

"I want to have a family with you," he explained.

"Um, okay, that's a strange request after what we did," she teased.

"I'm serious, babe."

"But years ago, you didn't want a family… What changed?"

"I have… and I know I want this with you, and only you."

"Why me?"

"Babe, you're the most amazing girl I know and I only want you to live this life with."

"What… I mean… are you sure? It's a big step."

"I know, and I want to take that step with you, and so many more."

"Well, I mean if you're all right with it, so am I," she said, with a nervous laugh.

Hovering over her, stroking her cheek. "Are you sure?" he asked, nervousness in his voice.

Nodding before answering. "Yes… I mean, yes, I'm in," she said, excitedly.

Before she could say anything else, he slammed his lips on hers. He didn't want her to have second thoughts. He was so happy that she wanted to take this step with him, and wondered if she was willing to take other steps with him.

***

As Kate and Luke pulled into a spot in a parking lot, he shut off the car. He rub her bare knee with a shaky and sweaty hand, as he looked out the windshield up at the courthouse. He turned his head when he felt a squeeze on his hand. He could see the worried expression on Kate's face.

"Are you okay?" she asked.

He nervously laughed. "Yeah, sorry, I didn't think I would do this,"

Luke explained.

"Oh, come on, you wanted to take the next step and this is the next step before we have a family," Kate teased.

"I know...It's just a big leap," he said, swallowing hard.

"Don't worry, I'll be right by your side," Kate encouraged.

"Thanks, Kate," he said, before smiling at her.

"No problem, cowboy," she replied, smiling back at him.

Patting his leg. "Now, let's get this over with," she said, with a heavy sigh.

Luke still couldn't believe they were doing this as he stared at her in her spring dress. He wished he could have bought her a better dress, but she didn't want to be too dressed up for this life changing event and she didn't want anything special. As she was about to get out of the car, he lightly gripped her wrist and tugged her back in. She furrowed her brow and looked at him with concern.

"Don't tell me you're getting cold feet," she teased.

"No, I just forgot to give you something," he said, with a nervous smile.

He pulled out a small, black leather notebook from the side of his seat and give it to her. She looked at it.

"What's this?"

"It's a journal that you left behind. It's where you kept all your song lyrics and our memories," he answered.

He watched as her hand slid over the cover with a big rubber band holding it closed. "I want you to keep doing that as we do everything together...I want you to record everything," he said.

"Everything?" she questioned.

He laughed nervously. "Well, I guess some things you could leave out unless you want to write about our sexual adventures."

***

She closed her eyes as she tightly hugged the notebook against her chest. She didn't realize she had left this behind when she left, which would explain why she couldn't find her song lyrics. Opening her eyes slowly, she was actually happy that Luke had it this whole time as she didn't want someone else to find it and destroy it as he had to her hopes and dreams. She shuddered at the thought of that man. Before Luke could ask what was wrong, she decided to hide her concerns with a smile.

"Okay, now, let's get this going. I didn't dress up for nothing," she teased.

***

Luke was hoping not to do this, but he did tell her he wanted to take every step with her, and this was the next one. Getting out of the car, she quickly wrapped her arms around his, as he stuffed his hands in his pockets. He couldn't believe he was doing this, as he stared up at the courthouse. Soon, the sound of a small plane engine caught his attention. He watched as a few people jumped out of it. His body began to shake more as he watched them fall, but before they got too close to the ground, they opened their chutes. He wanted to back away from this as his body shook more, but Kate was leading him like a nervous horse not wanting to go into a trailer.

Kate soon steered him away from the front of the courthouse as they made their way by it. As they got closer to their destination, he could see a small plane waiting in the field of a small airport. A man standing near the plane, talking to a couple of other people soon turned his attention on Kate and Luke. The man started to walk toward them.

"Kate... Luke, you made it!" he called out.

Kate let go of Luke's arm and run over to him to give him a hug. "So good to see you, Doug," she greeted.

Luke joined them as Doug changed his attention from Kate to him.

"Hey, man, never thought in a million years I would see you here," Doug joked.

Luke looked around. "Me either," he said, nervously.

"Don't worry, bud, I'll take good care of both you."

"I hope so."

Kate and Doug laughed before turning it to a conversation. Luke didn't catch a single word as his mind raced wondering why he would be stupid enough to do something like this.

What was I thinking?

***

Luke had a death grip on the bar on the wall of the plane and the bench he was sitting in. Each time the plane rocked, he swallowed hard and screwed his eyes shut. Eventually, he would open them when he felt Kate trying to reassure him.

"It'll be okay, Luke," she said.

"If you say so," Luke said, nervously.

"Don't worry, Doug won't let anything happen to us," she reassured.

"That's not what I'm worried about." The plane hit more turbulence and rocked harder. "I'm more afraid of the fall," he said, nervously, gripping harder.

Kate leaned in. "We're doing this together. I'll be right by your side," she said, to help.

Before he could complain anymore, she brought his face close to hers and kissed him. Even though he was afraid of heights, when she kissed him he felt as if he was on the clouds. She slowly pulled away as his heart started to slow down.

"Better?" she asked.

"Better."

"Good, because this is our drop-off point," she said, with a smile.

Before he could say anything else, he heard someone shuffling around the back of the plane. He looked over to see Doug standing there after opening the door.

"Are you guys ready?" he shouted.

Before he could tell Doug no and to go to hell, Kate had forced him to his feet. She kept pushing him toward the door until eventually she was standing right next to him. He was watching her until his eyes went over to the opening. He practically leapt backwards like he received an electric shock.

"I don't think I can do this!" he yelled over the plane's engine.

"Are you sure!" Kate shouted back.

"Yes!"

"Okay, then… Come here and give me a hug before I jump!"

Luke cautiously walked over and wrapped his arms around her. He felt her mouth near his ear.

"I'm sorry!" she yelled.

"For what?"

"This!"

Before he knew it, she leaned back and they both fell out of the plane.

"Kate!" he screamed.

He tried to get a death grip on her, but she somehow squirmed out of his hands and arms. He was only a few feet from her before looking down.

"Hey! Look at me!" she called.

His eyes slowly moved from the approaching ground to her. She reached out and held his hand.

"This is amazing!" she shouted.

"It is," he said to himself.

His moment with Kate was ruined when Doug showed up next to Kate. He used hand signals to show it was about time to pull their chutes. Kate smiled before letting go of Luke's hand. Luke watched as Kate shot up into the sky when her chute opened. He smiled as he couldn't believe that they did this before pulling his cord. Eventually, he shot up as well. As he drifted down, he admired the view, realizing he would have missed it, if it wasn't for Kate being Kate.

Looking at the ground, he could see it slowly getting closer. He prepared himself as they had told him during the training to land on his feet. As he stumbled along, he eventually was able to stand as his parachute collapse behind him. Looking around, he was wondering where Kate was. Without warning, he was tackled down to the ground, wrapping an arm around Kate as she kissed him. She pulled away first, sitting astride him, her arms up, shouting a victory cry.

"Not bad for not using large garbage bags like we used to," Kate teased, with a laugh.

Luke laughed as he recalled how many times they tried jumping off their houses, only using large, black garbage bags as parachutes. Even though he was afraid of heights back then, Kate made it easier to do until he broke his arm in the process. He recalled how much his parents yelled at him when he came home with a cast and missed out on some of the farm work, but he didn't care. Everything with Kate was worth it.

***

As they drove onto their next destination, Luke kept thinking about what Kate did to make him jump out of the plane. He was still laughing at himself for being such a big wuss. He looked over to see her looking out the window. His eyes wandered down to her leg as he enjoyed feeling her smooth leg. A smirk appeared on his face as he slowly moved his hand up, pushing her spring dress away. As he looked back at the road, he could see from the corner of his eye how a teasing smile appeared on her face. His hand continued to slide up as his heart pounded harder. He was almost to his destination until a sound caught his attention as an acoustic guitar was being strummed on the radio.

One day you got up and left me behind

I wished you'd asked if I mind...

In an instant, he practically leapt out of his chair and shut off the radio. Then he pretended as if nothing had happened as he could feel eyes on him. Peeking over, he could see Kate just eying him suspiciously.

"What was that about?" she asked.

"Was what?"

"Where you almost ripped the knob off the radio?"

"Huh?"

"Wow, okay... be weird then."

He watched as she crossed her arms and stared out the window. Biting his lower lip, he hated having her be like this, but he didn't want her to find out his secret. Putting a smile on his face, he shook her knee.

"Hey, how about we stop by and see my sis at work after this next thing?" he offered.

"Okay," she muttered.

Letting out a sigh, he couldn't believe he was even a wuss about telling her, but he didn't feel ready yet. It wasn't the right time. As he continued to drive, he hated the dead silence between them. He stroked her knee with his thumb as a way to feel connected with her. At the moment, it was all he needed.

***

As the big bull bucked, he sent the man riding him flying through the air before he fell hard on his side. The sound of his shoulder cracking under his weight was heard within earshot. As the other men rushed to help the fallen man, Luke and Kate look on. Luke smiled and looked over at Kate as she looked back.

"So, what do you think?" he asked.

"You really want to do this?"

"Yeah, why not?"

"Don't you think this is a bit too dangerous?"

"And skydiving wasn't?"

"I'm sorry, Luke, I just don't want to see you get   hurt."

"I won't, knowing you're here."

"How am I supposed to insure your safety?"

He leaned in and gave her a quick kiss on her cheek. "Because you're my lucky charm," he quickly answered.

Before he walked away, Kate grabbed hold of his hand. He looked back and could see she was frightened.

"Please, don't do this," she begged.

Pulling her into his arms, he wrapped them tightly around her.

"Don't worry, babe, I'm coming back unharmed because I know you're finally here with me," he whispered in her ear.

Pulling away, he watched as her face changed from fear to content. Walking toward the gate, he jumped back when the bull kicked the wall. Letting out a nervous laugh, he thought he was crazy for doing these things, but it was what he had wanted to do for a while now, and with Kate back in his life, he knew he had the confidence to do them.

"Ready, Luke?" a man asked.

"Yep," he answered, before climbing up and over the wall to be seated on the bull.

Luke leaned over and patted the bull. "Easy, fellow," he said, trying to calm it.

The beast snorted before doing a little jerk. As he looked over at Kate, Luke's heart pounded harder, not because of the bull riding, but the thought of something bad happening. Getting situated on the creature, he nodded toward her to let her know everything was okay. Too bad, he didn't believe that himself. Raising his left hand, he signaled the other man that he was ready.

In an instant, the gate opened up and the bull started to run and buck. Luke gripped the rope as hard as he could to stay on the monster as it continued to try to get him off of its back.

As the creature continued its whirlwind actions, Luke started to enjoy it as his heart didn't beat as hard against his ribs. As he jerked around a few times, he couldn't help but laugh and shout.

Without warning, the beast jerked hard right and threw Luke off. Laying there, he laughed his ass off until he saw Kate's face hovering over him. In that moment, his eyes widened as her safety became his concern. In one quick move, he threw her over his shoulder and jumped over the nearest fence, as the bull charged head on into it. Luke looked back and saw how close the creature had come to Kate, as he slowly slid her to her feet. Turning his head to look at her, her hands were on his face as she looked him up and down. He could tell she was concerned about him, as a big ass grin appeared on his face, laughing before slamming his lips on hers. She tried pushing him away, but he made sure to hold her tight against him so she couldn't leave him again.

As he quickly pulled away when he heard a familiar sound on the overhead speakers. Kate was still stunned as she just stood there with her eyes closed.

"Time to go," he said quickly, tugging on her hand.

Eventually, she came to and followed him. He was happy she hadn't questioned what the rush was, but he didn't need her to hear the song that was playing. He couldn't believe how today was going, as it was almost ruined by a song that seemed to be playing a lot today. Clenching his jaw, he hoped that their next stop wouldn't have it.

***

After pulling into the back of his sister's realtor office, Luke put it in park and cupped Kate's face as he kissed her. His hand slid up her dress back to where he started earlier. Her moans were muffled against his lips as he listened to the sweet sounds of her enjoying his fingers moving in and out of her.

She pulled his hand away from her, and before he could question why she did that, she sat astride on his lap. He chuckled as he watched her work his belt buckle and jeans. Tilting his head back, fisting her hips, he enjoyed the welcoming warmth of her as she slowly slid down him. He vigorously thrust into her as she kissed and nibbled all over his face and neck. A song came on the radio that had the worst timing in the world, so he held her face close to him as his mouth was near her ear.

"Oh, Kate," he grunted.

"Luke," she whimpered.

His body shuddered from her saying his name like that, as the song seemed to end. He wasn't expecting it to be short, but before he knew it, he grunted, and air quickly escaped him as he bucked a few more times into her. As he calmed down, he listened to her whimper next to him. When he moved his face, he got a face full of her hair and didn't mind having it as he inhaled as much of her smell before blowing out to try to breathe normally.

"That was exhilarating," he said, sexily.

"I would say," she sighed.

She sat up and looked at him. "What was that about?" she teased, with a smirk.

"I just love feeling alive with you," he answered, with a big grin on his face.

She laughed. "Well, the feeling is mutual," she said, before getting off him.

She got out of the car as he fixed himself before going into his sister's office. He didn't want her to tease him about anything that they did prior to going in. He quickly wiped the sweat off his face as he felt it between her and him after their quickie. Getting out, he could see Kate waiting for him. Wrapping an arm around her, he pulled her in for another kiss before they walked through the back door.

Looking around, he spotted his sister down the hallway toward the front.

"Hey, Sis!" he called out.

"Luke!" she called back.

Kate pulled Luke so he could lean near her. "Hey, I'm going to quickly freshen up," she whispered.

"Okay, babe," he said, before planting a soft kiss on her cheek.

"Ah, get a room you two," CindyLou joked.

Kate left Luke's arm as she went into the nearby bathroom. Luke walked over to his sister.

"So, what have you two, lovebirds, been up to?" CindyLou teased, as Luke walked toward her.

"Oh, you know, some stuff."

"Well, with that big grin on your face, I would say you fuck...then you fuck some more and oh hey, some more fucking," she teased.

"Oh, come on, C," Luke said, rolling his eyes.

She pulled up his sleeve. "And what is this," she exclaimed, when she saw the bandage.

"Nothing," he quickly answered, before pulling his arm away from her.

"Doesn't seem like nothing... Luke, you need to slow down," CindyLou explained.

"I'm fine."

"I know you were given a second chance, but you need to be careful."

"I will," he grumbled.

***

Kate exited the bathroom and was about to join Luke and CindyLou, but something caught her attention from the corner of her eye. Walking into Luke's sister's office, she spotted some newspaper clippings in frames on her wall. She squinted her eyes as confusion soon swarmed her mind. She couldn't believe what she was seeing and reading. Her eyes finally fell onto a magazine on CindyLou's desk. Picking up the magazine, she stared at the front cover photo and her mind went blank. She turned and walked out of the office, still staring at the magazine. She could hear Luke and CindyLou still talking, but had no idea what they were saying. She slowly looked up as they continued their conversations as if she's not even there. Anger flow through her veins as she was about to blow.

***

Luke heard something flying through the air and stepped back with his arms shooting up to shield himself from what was being thrown at him. Looking in the direction that the magazine came from, he could see Kate standing there, her face as red as a tomato with tears welling up in her eyes.

"Kate?" he questioned, with concern in his voice.

"What the hell is that?" she asked, in an angry voice, pointing at the limp magazine.

Luke slowly looked down and saw the cover. Staring back him was a picture of him on the front cover of *Country Star* magazine. Closing his eyes, he wished that Kate hadn't seen it. Now, he'd need to explain it all to her. Before he could, he suddenly heard the song he had been hiding from Kate the whole time on the nearby radio.

One day you got up and left me behind

I wished you'd asked if I mind

Sweet, sweet Katelyn

Where have you been

I hope you found greener pastures

As I mope like a bastard

Landing in exotic lands

I still wonder where you've been

You went out for a new life

By becoming another's wife

Luke opened his eyes slowly and watched Kate. At first, she didn't notice and then the wheels started to turn in her head and her eyes were searching.

Are you happy sweet Katelyn

Where have you been

Please come back to me

So we could be.

As the song ended, Kate's eyes locked with his and he was terrified by what he saw in them. He cautiously walked toward her to see her as she was when he found her at the gas station.

"Kate," he said, softly.

Before he could touch her, she slapped his hand away.

"What the?" she asked.

Luke was hoping she hadn't heard any of the song, but he could tell she had and everything was clicking.

"That's your voice… what the hell was that song about?" she asked angrily, her voice shaking.

"Babe, it's just a song," he tried to explain.

Shutting her eyes, tears fell. "What is the song about?" she asked again, her voice really shaking.

Luke was both terrified and concerned about Kate as he could tell it was ripping her inside. He hadn't meant for it to do that. It was just a stupid song he came up with about her and was dumbass drunk one night at open mic at the bar and he fucking sang it. Shaking his head, he didn't know what he could do to help salvage the situation. Before he could say anything, Kate opened her eyes and just shook her head before turning and bolting. Luke was about to run after her, but he became so dizzy from his heart racing that he had to catch himself from falling.

"I'm okay!" he yelled when CindyLou tried to help.

"Okay," was all she said.

Slapping his forehead. "I'm so fucking stupid... what is wrong with me?" he asked, before he collapsed on the floor.

As he sat there, he covered his face with his hands, sobbing away.

What have I done...

***

Kate had no idea where she was going, but she needed to get away. Tears flew off her face as the wind whipped past her face. People tried to stop her to talk to her, but she kept pushing past them.

Luke, why...

***

Johnboy slowed his vehicle down and looked carefully down the road. Turning his car around, he drove down the road and found Kate walking along with her arms crossed. As he got next to her, he slowed and rolled down the passenger's window.

"Hey, Kate."

"Not now, Johnboy," she sniffled.

Stopping his car, he quickly got out of it to jog toward Kate. She started to walk briskly, and he did the same. Soon, he jogged backward with a big grin on his face.

"Oh, come on, Kate... It's me, your good old Johnboy," he teased.

"Sorry, Johnboy, not in the mood."

He put his hand out to stop her. She looked at him and he could tell she was still angry.

"Look, Kate, I know you're mad at Luke... Trust me, I would be too, but come on as a songwriter you should know better," Johnboy insisted.

She sighed. "I don't know what I'm angry about anyways," she said.

"Hey, I know it's a lot to take in, but he didn't mean to be hurtful," Johnboy explained.

"I just wish he had told me before."

"Trust me, knowing him, he probably didn't know how to explain it without doing any damage."

"True. He's always concerned with not hurting others."

"So, would you come back and let him explain it now?" Johnboy asked.

"Yeah."

"Good." He took off his suit jacket and wrapped it around her. "Because it's getting chilly and he will kill me if you get sick," Johnboy joked.

***

They walked back to his car, and Kate realized that Johnboy was right. She was freaking out over nothing. So what if Luke had become a country star?

"At least, one of us did," she whispered under her breath.

***

Luke hadn't stopped pacing at his place since he got there. His sister had told him to go home and she and Johnboy would go out and find Kate. He wished he was out there looking for her too, but he knew his sister was more concerned that he might end up not being much help. His chest hurt so much as his heart pounded hard against it and his head spun, but he couldn't sit and wait.

His head shot up when he heard a car pulling in and the headlights washed over the window. Tripping on the rug, he jumped over the coffee table, and raced for the door. He swung it open and only saw Johnboy standing there. Luke's heart dropped as his stomach twisted more. He figured that Johnboy was here to tell him bad news. Lowering his head, he banged it off the doorframe.

"I'm such a fucking asshole," he said, with a sob.

"I would say you are," Kate said.

Luke looked up and saw her walk around Johnboy with his suit jacket still wrapped around her.

"Kate," he said, in disbelief.

She turned and handed Johnboy his jacket before looking at Luke and placing her hands on her hips.

"You have a lot of explaining to do, cowboy," she said, sternly.

"Yes, I do," he said, with a heavy swallow.

Johnboy looked between them before breaking the silence. "Well, I'm just…yeah," he said, before leaving.

Kate made her way into the house as Luke watched her. He didn't want to spook her again as he didn't like having that feeling when she left him. It was the most excruciating pain he'd had ever felt and he had a lot of broken bones growing up.

She slowly sat on the couch and patted the spot next to her. He made a gradually move toward it and sat. His stomach twisted and turned if it were being wrung out. Swallowing hard again, he waited for her to say something as she stared at the floor and clasped her hands together on her lap. He could see she was really thinking about something.

"Time to clear the air," she said, quietly.

"Yes."

"First off, I want to apologize…"

"Oh, Kate, you don't need to. I totally understand why you ran off," he said, quickly.

"Not that," she said, looking at him.

"Oh."

"I meant the time you asked about what happened and I freaked out on you."

"Oh, Kate, you don't have to tell me. It was wrong of me to put my nose where it didn't belong."

"I figure if we're going to try a life together again, then I guess we need to be honest with each other."

"Um, okay."

"Luke." She took a deep breath before continuing. "When I left here, I ended up in New York City, where a guy I met promised me the chance of being a famous country singer," she explained.

"Okay."

"Well, I should have known it was a lie as he despised country music, but I was young and naïve, believing the world was like this small town."

"Oh, Kate," he said, holding her hands in his.

"Well, at first, it was a great feeling with all the attention, but soon the illusion disappeared and his mask was removed."

She turned to look into Luke's eyes. He saw such sadness that made his eyes well up.

"I was nothing but arm candy for him out in public, but in private, I was just his punching bag," she finished.

Luke brought her tight against him as she began to cry into his chest.

"I'm so sorry, Luke. I should have just come home," she cried.

"It's okay, babe. You're home now, and I'll make sure you're taken care of," he hushed.

Pushing away from him, they locked eyes again as she sniffled a few times.

"So, tell me about becoming a country star," she said.

He nervously laughed. "Well, it was by pure accident actually. I wasn't planning on it," he explained.

"What?"

"Well, it's a silly story…After you left, I couldn't function anymore and almost lost the farm if it hadn't been for CindyLou keeping it up."

"Oh, Luke," she cried, fisting his flannel shirt.

"So, one night, being drunk off my ass on open mic night, I made the mistake of taking a seat on stage. Before I knew it, I was singing the song that had been playing over and over in my head after you left. After I was finished licking my wounds, I was about to go home to drown my sorrows some more until an agent walked up to me. He offered me a contract and everything. Of course, at the time, I wasn't functional, so CindyLou took care of all of it. Next morning, I found out I was a country star."

Pulling Kate tighter against him, he said, his voice shaking "Oh, babe, I tried looking for you to share in the stardom with me."

"Really? Why?"

Pulling away from her, he explained. "Because it was our dream to be country singers together and you were my everything."

"You mean you never moved on from me, even after I broke your heart?"

"No, you were the only girl for me. You were the Joan to my Johnny. You were the Cher to my Sonny. You were the lone star in my night sky… Kate, you didn't break my heart, you took it with you," Luke said, sadly, stroking her cheek.

Rubbing her nose against his. "I'm so sorry, Luke. Please forgive me."

"Of course, babe, I will… just as long as you never leave me again," he begged.

"No…No, I would never do that to you ever again."

"Oh, babe… I fucking love you so much."

"Ditto," she teased.

Luke's mouth covered hers as he wanted to show her how much he needed and wanted her. She pulled him down on her as she laid back. His hands quickly undressed her as her hands had him ready to enter her. Their moans and groans were muffled by their kissing as Luke rocked into her hard and fast. His heart pounded hard and loud in his ears, but he ignored it as he never wanted to let Kate go, ever again.

Pulling away, he ordered huskily "I'm not going to let you up until I have my fucking fill."

She pulled him back to her lips as her tongue twirled around his, causing chills to run across his skin.

I fucking love her…

CHAPTER SIX

"Ow!" Kate yelled, as she lay on her stomach.

Clenching her jaw, she listened the needle in the tattoo gun buzz. She couldn't believe she was doing this, but Luke wanted to do it. If she didn't know any better, she would have guessed this was a bucket list of some sort. Coming back from her thoughts when she felt a squeeze on her hand, she looked up to see Luke looking very concerned. She had to keep him from jumping the tattoo artist as he was ready to punch the guy for hurting her. He had already had his done, and she reminded him that it did hurt.

"You know you didn't need to do this," he said, softly.

"I know, but I was jealous," she joked.

Rolling his eyes. "Well, you didn't have to get a big tattoo like that."

"I know, but I liked it."

"Babe, you're so fucking hot," he whispered, before leaning in to kiss her.

She laughed before screwing her eyes shut when the tattoo artist did more work on her back. Opening them quickly.

"It's okay, I'm okay," she reassured Luke.

He relaxed a little and sighed as he sat back. She could tell he didn't like this, but at least he wasn't punching the tattoo artist.

***

As they left the tattoo parlor, Luke had never let go of her and planted kisses whenever he could. She laughed as she recalled how he used to be like this back in the day.

"So, how are you going to explain your tattoo to the church people when we sing this Sunday?" he teased.

She turned so he could see her back as she pointed at it.

"Hey, it's religious, it's angel wings," she joked.

Luke pulled the back of her tank top down a little more and saw more of the angel wings she had tattooed on her back.

"So, what made you get those?" he teased with a smile.

She turned to look at him. "Because I'm an angel," she flirted back.

He laughed, shaking his head.

"What? I am an angel, unlike you who copied me," she said, with amusement in her voice.

"I didn't copy you," he defended himself.

"Then why did you go with angel wings on your back, too."

"They're not angel wings."

"Prove it," she teased, crossing her arms.

"Fine," he said, with a smile, pulling his shirt off and turning around.

He shuddered at the feel of her hand rubbing against his new tattoo on his back. He let her examine it for a while, enjoying her touch on his sensitive skin.

"A bird?" she questioned.

"Not just any bird… it's a phoenix."

"Why a phoenix?"

"Because, like a phoenix that rises up from the ashes, I was given a second chance," he said, quietly.

She slowly turned him around and he could see the concern in her eyes as tears threatened to fall. Stroking her face, he didn't want the tattoo as something to harm her.

"I'm sorry," she said, bowing her head.

Cupping her chin and lifting it up. "Don't be, I'm happy you're back with me," he said, with a smile.

Before she could object anymore, he covered her mouth with his. He didn't want her to worry about such things. It was a stupid idea for the tattoo, but for some reason, he picked it out. He guessed his mind and heart wanted a physical reminder of his second chance coming back into his life.

***

Kate kept staring out at the church crowd behind a big, velvet curtain. Clenching onto it, like a life preserver, her body shook.

"Why did I agree to this?" she asked herself.

"What was that?" Luke asked from behind.

She turned to see him standing there in his Sunday's best and holding his guitar. If her mind wasn't on the group out there, she would be undressing him with her eyes. Shaking her head to rid such impure thoughts from her mind while in the house of God, she let out a slow, shaky breath.

"I can't do this," she said.

"Yeah, you can. We've done this before," Luke said with a smile, rubbing her arm.

"Yeah, but that was long ago. It's been so long and I think I might be rusty."

"Oh, come on, Kate, you sound amazing in the car and in the shower," he said, before getting tight against her with his arm wrapped around her waist. "Well, when I'm not tongue fucking your mouth," he said, with a tease.

Her jaw dropped with nothing coming out of it as he winked at her.

"Maybe I shouldn't have said that, now the duet will only be me," he joked.

"I can't believe you're making me hot and bothered while we're here," she said.

"Well, maybe this will help," he said, leaning down.

Before she could respond, he placed a gentle, long kiss on her lips. As he pulled away, she felt as light as air and slowly opened her eyes, staring at him as his grin grew bigger.

"Did that work?" he teased.

She nodded her head.

"You sure?" he laughed.

"Two can play at this game," she said, before pulling him down. "Wait until we get back to your car and I'll show what heaven feels like," she whispered in his ear.

Pulling away, she watched as his mouth hung open and his eyes went wide. Patting on his chest, she smiled.

"I win," she said, quietly, before turning around.

Laughing to herself, she could feel his eyes were stuck on her as she walked out onto the stage. She took her seat on a stool that was placed there for her as the crowd clapped. A few seconds later, Luke finally showed up, waving a hand as the crowd erupted into cheers. She laughed as she saw how red his face was. He took his seat next to her and fumbled with the guitar on his lap. Her smile grew bigger as she loved how she got him hot and bothered.

"Ready," he said, after clearing his throat.

Kate loved how his voice cracked as he must have been really bothered by what she said to him behind the curtain. As the crowd started to quiet down, he began to strum the guitar. Kate smiled as she recalled the chords and what song they were going to sing. It was a classic, but a good one to sing.

"Now, I heard there was a secret chord…" Kate began to sing the song *Hallelujah*.

***

As Luke played the guitar, he watched as Kate sang with her eyes closed. His heart beating hard against his chest as he couldn't believe how much her singing affected him. Chills ran down his spine, and all he could do was stare at the angel next to him. When it came to the chorus, he joined in, singing right along with her. Their voices mixed together perfectly as they used to when they sang together. That was one of the reasons why people always wanted them to sing at events. After the chorus, it was his turn to sing. He looked down at his guitar, from the corner of his eye he could see Kate watching him sing his part.

"She broke your throne, and she cut your hair…" he continued to sing before looking at her. "And from your lips she drew the hallelujah," he sang, staring into her eyes.

Right on cue, she sang the chorus with him without removing her eyes from his. Surprisingly, with his heart beating faster and harder as ever, he didn't feel the usual dizziness, but had such a great feeling singing with Kate again. His body felt alive after being in a deep slumber. He hoped that this would never end, but realized they were close to the end.

"Hallelujah," they both sang, ending the song.

They stared at each other, as their seemed to be silence and it was just them in the room. Luke liked how it always felt like that, but he knew there was a crowd and they were clapping and cheering, but they were too preoccupied with each other that they didn't notice.

Eventually, Kate was the first to look away and smile at the crowd. Luke kept his eyes on her as she waved to a few people. He wasn't the type that enjoyed big groups of people, but with Kate by his side, he didn't feel too awkward. It was hard when the agency wanted him to tour and do his songs. He panicked every time he had to go in front of a crowd. The only way he got through it was when he closed his eyes and pretended Kate was by his side, singing with him like now.

As his eyes wandered down her body, he saw her Sunday's best was snugged against the curves of her body. Biting his lower lip, her comment from earlier echoed through his head, causing his dress pants to become tighter. Lucky for him, he had his guitar to hide it from the crowd. When she looked at him, he knew it was time to take her up on her offer. Before anyone could request an encore, he tugged her hand and pulled her away from the stage through the backdoor. Locating his Charger out in the field under a tree, he spun on his heels and whipped her up over his shoulder, making quick his escape to their destination.

Once at his Charger, he slid her down on to her feet. She leaned forward to kiss him, but he make sure there was distance as he opened the car door and climbed in. She looked in with her brow furrowed.

"What are you doing?" she asked, with confusion in her voice.

As he lay on his back with an arm behind his head. "Well, you promise me the feeling of heaven. So, take me to heaven, angel," he teased, before he held up his hand. "I'm waiting."

She smiled before climbing in. Astride him, she began to passionately kiss him and slowly help remove his shirt and undershirt. They laughed as they became goofy, trying to remove each other's clothes in the backseat of the Charger. Luke started to feel like a couple of high schoolers parking as they used to when they were younger. The song by Meatloaf popped in his head called *Objects In The Rear-View Mirror May Appear Closer Than They Are.*

I'm in the back seat with my Julie like a Romeo...out of the back seat now, just like an angel rising up from a tomb.

***

Curled up on her side against Luke, Kate listened as Luke hummed the song, his fingers lightly rubbing her arm. They were still in the backseat of the Charger and relaxing after she made him feel as if he'd died and went to heaven. Closing her eyes, she was about to drift off to sleep, but her eyes sprung open when she heard him say something. Sitting up, she looked at his face and could see he was serious about it.

"What?" she asked, still shocked.

"Marry me," he begged, softly, nervousness in his voice.

All Kate could do was stare at him. He became twitchy as he was about to sit up as well. She placed her hand on his chest to keep him there. Blinking a few times, her heart fluttered as her mind whirled with so many thoughts.

"I'm sorry," she started, with a nervous laugh. "I thought you just asked me to marry you."

"I did."

***

Luke hated seeing her like this. She had never taken so long to answer him about anything until now. He saw the turmoil in her eyes as her hand went up to her forehead and she closed her eyes. He sat up and cupped her face to have her look at him.

"Are you okay?" he asked.

She nodded and stared at him. Their eyes locked.

"I'm so sorry, it was stupid of me to ask," he apologized.

"No, it wasn't. I'm just shocked, I guess."

"Why?"

"Because you never cared if we got married or not and also you want to have a child. I guess it was just a bit too much for me to take in."

"Hey, babe, we don't have to if you don't want to… it was just a crazy thought and I was in the moment," he said, nervously.

He was about to brush it off, but she brought his face back so his eyes were on hers.

"Yes," she said, quietly.

"What?"

"I said, yes, you, silly cowboy," she exclaimed.

He hugged her tight as he couldn't believe she had said yes. He was sure she wouldn't want to, because for many years before she left, he wanted to propose to her, but he was too nervous. Even when it was a good time, he just chickened out.

Closing his eyes, they laughed together. He loved seeing the sparkle of excitement in her eyes and loved how she was no longer the shadow of the person before. She even gained some weight, which he was glad about, seeing as she was too thin and she was almost skin and bone. Soon, her hot breath was against his ear.

"I love you, Luke," she whispered.

"I love you, too, Kate," he replied.

***

Luke revved the engine of a beat-up Oldsmobile. He smiled as he looked over to his side and saw Kate fixing her helmet before getting situated in her beat-up Chevy. Luke laughed as he couldn't believe they were going to do a demolition derby together at the fair. He looked around and could see all their competitors. He was a little afraid of Kate getting hurt, but she reminded him of all the times they did bumper cars together. Luke knew he wasn't going to win so he gave in.

He looked over at Kate again and she gave him two thumbs up to show she'd be okay. He mouthed the words 'I love you' as she mouthed back 'ditto'. He laughed again as he looked out where the windshield window should be. His nerves were on high alert as the adrenaline rushed through his veins. His body shook and his heart palpitated. Clenching his jaw, he tried to calm his body, not because he was excited, but because he was afraid of Kate getting hurt, which caused his symptoms to act up.

Before he could change his mind about Kate being there, a loud air horn sounded. His car jerked forward as he was attempting to protect Kate from most of the hits. Metal smashed against more metal. Dirt and mud flew everywhere as dented vehicles crawled through the area to hit other vehicles. Eventually, Kate escaped his protective shield and raced around in the dirt and mud. He laughed as he listened to her shouting and hollering. He eventually joined in the fun and let go of all his worries. The song *I Want Crazy* by Hunter Hayes played loudly over the speakers. Luke laughed harder as he couldn't believe the perfect timing of the song as he and Kate had fun in the demolition derby.

***

Luke leaned against the railing as he watched Kate on a mechanical bull, loving watching her as she did her best to stay on it. Of course, it was easy for her compared to him bull riding a real bull. Eventually, she's bucked off. Luke vaulted over the railing and ran to her. Crouching down, he examined her to make sure she was okay. She let out a big laugh as she smiled up at him.

"I'm okay," she said.

He smiled back, helping her to stand. Before they're situated, she was already tugging him to follow her. They hadn't really taken a break since they got out of the derby. They had practically done everything in the fair, except one. Luke looked up and saw the Ferris wheel.

He soon detoured her from wherever she was going and headed toward the Ferris wheel. He slid some money into the guy's hand and lean in to whisper something. After the guy nod his head in agreement, Luke turned and saw Kate giving him a suspicious look. He just smiled and led her to an open bench on the ride.

The attendant closed the bar across their lap and went to the controls. Kate watched with interest, and Luke could see she had figured out that it would be only them on this ride. It went around a few times until it slowly stopped at the top. Kate rolled her eyes as Luke act surprised.

"Oh no, we stopped for some reason," he said, innocently.

"Oh, yeah, what a surprise," she teased.

Putting his arm around her shoulders, he pulled her tight against him before looking ahead of them, pointing toward the sky.

"Well, I hope you'll like this surprise," he said, softly.

In an instant, the sky lit up with explosions and different colors. Luke looked over and could see her watching the fireworks in amazement. He thought she would like being able to watch the fireworks up this high. Usually, they would sit on top of one of the stables to watch the fireworks, but seeing that he had the money from his stardom, he was able to make this possible. Just one of the perks of being a country star. After placing a kiss on her cheek, he moved toward her ear.

"You're amazing, babe," he whispered.

Pink showed up on her cheeks as a small smile spread on her face. She looked up at him with those long, tantalizing eyelashes with those bright, hazel eyes. He brushed back her wheat-colored hair and glad it wasn't dry and broken anymore, but soft and fine like a baby's hair.

"Shouldn't you be watching the fireworks, cowboy," she teased.

"Sorry, I saw something more amazing," he laughed, before turning his attention back to the fireworks.

"Well, if you think I'm amazing now… I have a better surprise for you," she whispered in his ear.

"What's that, babe?" he asked, not removing his eyes from the fireworks.

She leaned more in. "I'm pregnant," she whispered.

As she leaned back, he turned his head with his eyes wide.

"You are?" he asked, still in shock.

She nodded and bit her lower lip.

Before he knew it, he slammed his lips on hers and kissed her a few times.

"Oh, babe, you are amazing," he said, excitedly.

His mouth covered hers and he held her tight against him. He never wanted to let her go. So many thoughts whirled in his head, as he didn't know what to do first. As he pulled away, he had almost forgotten what else he wanted to do tonight.

"Hey, let's sneak into old man Jerry's place and skinny dip in his lake," Luke suggested.

Kate laughed. "Are you serious? Right now?" she asked.

"Yeah, why not?"

"Wow, are you in a hurry to finish your bucket list or something," she teased.

Luke froze as he didn't know what to say to her. She broke his stillness when she lightly slapped his chest.

"Sounds like fun, cowboy. Let's do it," she said, with a big smile.

"Alright, let's finished this ride first, darling," he said, in his southern drawl.

Holding her close to him again, he brushed a kiss in her hair. Panic rushed through him, but soon disappeared as the ride started to go again. Closing his eyes, he listened to her laugh and squeezed his knee when the ride dropped rapidly, her words echoing in his head.

Wow, are you in a hurry to finish your bucket list or something...

***

CindyLou sat down at the bar as the bartender placed her drink before

her.

"Thanks, Mick."

As she took a sip, she could feel someone sitting next to her, turned to look at them, and examined him from head to toe. She could tell he didn't live around here as he seemed too prepped and pampered. Turning her body to face him, she put her hand out.

"Howdy, stranger, what brings you to these parts?" she flirted.

"Business," he grumbled.

"Well, well, I'm a business woman myself... well, realtor mostly, but still a business woman," she said, playfully.

He looked over at her, examining her before turning his head. "I'm not looking for a prostitute, toots."

"A what... Oh, no, I think you have the wrong impression, I'm not that type of business woman."

"Then why are you talking to me?"

"Because..." she squeezed his knee, leaning forward. "We could always have some fun while you're in town," she said, seductively.

He raised an eyebrow. "Really?"

"Really."

He smiled and she smiled back.

***

"I can't believe we're doing this," Luke said, nervously, removing his shirt.

"I know, it's crazy," Kate laughed, pulling down her jeans.

Kate stood there only in her panties and bra, as Luke licked his lips and walked over to her. He pulled her tight against him with his hand on her lower back, exhaling sharply when her hands touched his chest.

"Oh, babe, you look like a fucking sexy goddess," he whispered.

Her hands slid down his chest, slowly, his abs tightening when her fingers slid down them. Resting his forehead against her head, he watched as she quickly unbuckled his belt and undid his jeans. His head whipped back as he sucked in air quickly when her hand slid in and gripped his hardened need. She began to stroke him as his breathing became shaky.

"Oh babe, you're so fucking amazing… I can't seem to get enough of you."

She stood on her tippy toes and her bottom lip brushed his lips.

"Well, cowboy, you can have more of me in the water," she teased.

His eyes sprung open, his arms searching out for her as she turned and ran from him. He quickly followed as she left a trail of her bra and panties behind, attempting to remove the rest of his clothing along the way. As he got closer to the lake, he heard a splash and knew she was in the water already. He stood on the edge and saw her treading water, waiting for him. He smiled before jumping in, and she laughed as she tried to block the water splashing her.

Raking his hair back, he watched a smirk appeared on her face, and before he knew it, she was splashing him with water. He put his hands out to shield himself, but it was no use, so he started to splash her back. They laughed and continued splashing each other until he made his way close to her and covered her mouth with his. She wrapped her legs above his hips as he treaded water for both of them, his groans muffled as her hardened nipples brushed against his chest.

As she continued to passionately kiss him and let her tongue play with his, he swam them both over to the pier, holding on to it as he pressed her against the ladder. Her arms slid away from being around his neck and held onto the pier behind her, as he trailed feathery kisses along her jawline and neck, slowly sliding into her, hearing a soft whimper escape her lips.

Wrapping an arm around her waist, he pressed his face into the nape of her neck and began to rock into her, listening to her softly moaning and the water lightly splashing.

"Oh, God," he grunted.

"Oh, Luke… right there," she groaned.

Clenching his jaw, he tried to refrain from thrusting hard or fast into her, wanting to take his sweet time showing her how much he loved her as her arms snaked around his neck while she nibbled and licked his ear.

"Luke, harder," she begged, in his ear.

Letting go of all the worries that were weighing on his mind, he did as she asked. He grunted with her sounds of moans and whimpers as their passion lapped the water against the pier.

"You like that," Luke asked, huskily in her ear before kissing it.

"Yes… keep going… I'm almost there," she pleaded.

"Oh, babe, you're so fucking hot," he said, before thrusting hard into her.

"Yeah… keeping talking," she begged.

"Your tits feel so fucking amazing against me."

"What else?"

"Oh, babe, you make me fucking hard every time you're around me."

"Mmm… I love having your hard cock inside me."

"Do you? Well, let me go balls deep then."

He pushed hard into her, as far as he could go and felt her convulse around him as he bucked a few more times inside her. Holding her close to him, he could feel her body shaking as she calmed down. He let out a laugh.

"That was amazing," he said, in a shaky voice.

"Yeah, it was," she said, with a sigh.

He started to kiss, and she let his tongue enter her mouth. They were going to go again, but a sound caught their attention. Luke squinted his eyes as if he were trying to see in the dark. He heard a giggle again from a woman, and saw her leading a man down toward them. Luke and Kate both quickly swam to the shore and got out of the water. Luke rushed and picked up their clothing with Kate right behind him. They found bushes to hide behind as they quickly got dressed until Kate grabbed Luke's arm and started to squeeze it hard. Luke looked over, wondering what was wrong. Her eyes were as wide as saucers and he could see in the dimly lit area that all the color had left her face.

"What's wrong?" he whispered.

"It's him," she said, her voice shaking with fear.

He looked at her hand on his arm and felt how much her body was following her voice.

"Who?" he asked.

Kate looked over at him, eventually it all clicked when he saw the terrified look in her eyes. As he looked at the guy, he felt the burning anger flowing through his veins and was about to go over there and kick his ass, but Kate's squeeze caused him to look at her again.

"Luke, we need to get CindyLou away from him," she said, quietly.

Luke looked back and recognized his sister with the asshole. He turned to look at Kate.

"Stay here," he ordered.

Before Kate could stop him, he walked out of the bushes, quickly putting his shirt on. As he walked nonchalantly toward his sister, she slowly turned her attention from the asshole to him.

"Luke?" she questioned.

"Hey, CindyLou, I've been looking all over for you," Luke said, with a smile.

"You have?"

"Yeah, I thought you said to meet you inside."

CindyLou just stared at him with a confused expression on her face.

"Where are my manners?" Luke said, before moving toward his sister. "I should hug my big sister as I haven't seen you forever," he lied.

As he hugged CindyLou, she went stiff, even more confused.

"Hey, we need to go...like now," he whispered in her ear.

She pulled away and he could see she understood what he was saying.

"Oh, Luke, I'm so sorry, I totally forgot."

She looked over at the guy. "I'm so sorry, but I had a prior engagement," she apologized.

"It's okay," he mumbled, before walking away.

Once the guy was gone, CindyLou turned to look at Luke and smacked him.

"Now, can you tell me what's going on?" she asked, angrily.

Before Luke could answer, a rustling of the bushes caught both of their attention.

"Sorry, CindyLou, but that was my ex," Kate explained, with sadness in her voice.

"Your ex?" CindyLou asked.

Kate looked away and wrapped her arms around herself. Luke shot CindyLou a look to drop it before moving toward Kate and pulling her against him.

"It's okay, he won't hurt you anymore," he vowed.

Kate sniffled a few times. "I know," she said, quietly.

Luke pulled away to see if she was okay. "Hey, let's go home," he said, before looking around. "I think we had enough fun tonight."

Wrapping his arm around her shoulders, they walked back to his car in silence. He hated this, as it was very rare when there was silence between them unless they were sleeping, which they hardly did when they were together. Luke pulled her tight against him, as she leaned in to cry quietly into his shirt.

***

CindyLou stood there, unsure what had happened.

"Hey, is anyone going to explain what's going on?"

No one answered.

"Guys?" she called out.

Eventually, she threw her arms down and stomped away.

"Unbelievable," she muttered under her breath.

***

"Hey, I'm going to take a shower," Kate mumbled, wrapping Luke's flannel shirt tightly around her.

"Okay, I'll be in in a bit."

He watched as she left the bedroom with her face tear-stained, hating that she was feeling like this. He had to pull the car over when she started to cry harder. She curled into a tight ball that it was hard to uncurl her so he could soothe her. Even though her bruises were fading, he could imagine she still had haunting injuries in her heart and mind.

Coming back from that awful memory, he waited until he could hear the shower running. He made his way over to a small drawer on the night stand and pulled out a piece of yellow stationery paper that was folded multiple times. Slowly, unfolding it, it revealed a list on it. Picking up the pen off the night stand, he searched the list and found what he was looking for. He crossed out the line that said:

Kiss Kate on top of the Ferris wheel.

As he examined the list, he saw some of the items were crossed out, such as getting a tattoo, riding a bull, and skydiving with Kate. A smile slowly spread on his face as he saw toward the bottom two other items.

Have a family with Kate.

Marry Kate.

His eyes wandered up the list to the top where it read:

Bucket List

There were a lot of items listed that weren't crossed out, but he knew he would soon have them crossed out as he continued working through the list with Kate. There were some on there that he thought maybe he was too drunk when he wrote this list out after he received the concerning news. Licking his lips, he realized a lot of them had something to do with Kate. He laughed to himself, as he hadn't been sure that she would come back to him when he made this list. It was some drunken man's wish list, and now it was coming true. Sighing, he still couldn't believe his luck, but then his stomach started to twist as he thought what would happened once he completed the list.

Shaking such bad thoughts from his mind, he quickly crossed out:

Do Demolition Derby.

Sing with Kate.

Skinny dip and make love to Kate.

Satisfied with his work, he quickly refolded the paper and stuffed it under the other items in the drawer, and ripped off his shirt as he made his way to the bathroom, not wanting Kate to be alone with her thoughts.

He slowly slipped in behind her, wrapping her in his arms as he began to rock them. Planting kisses on her shoulder, he watched her face as it showed that she was starting to feel better. He began humming a tune and then sang the lyrics of *Your Guardian Angel* by the Red Jumpsuit Apparatus.

"When I see you smile… Tears run down my face," he started to sing.

She slowly turned around in his arms as she lay her head on his shoulder. He continued to sing and watch her as a smile gradually appeared on her face.

"I'll be there for you through it all, even if saving you sends me to heaven," he finished, before starting to hum the tune to her.

"Thanks, Luke," she said, quietly.

"No, problem, babe."

Tightening his hold on her, he never wanted to let her go again.

CHAPTER SEVEN

Kate let out a giggle as Luke kissed and nibbled along her jawline. He had set her down on the counter and was between her legs as his flannel shirt she was wearing fell open to reveal she was only wearing a bra and panties. Her hands brushed against his bare chest as he stood there only in his jeans. They were going to make breakfast, but got distracted with each other.

Luke tilted his head back, groaning and rolling his eyes when the back door swung open. He watched as CindyLou walked around the corner and let out a scream before covering her eyes.

"You guys ever heard of keeping it in the bedroom?"

"Ever heard of knocking?" Luke asked, before fixing himself.

"Hi, CindyLou," Kate said, sweetly.

"Hi Kate," CindyLou said, smiling, before looking over at Luke. "See, at least Kate knows how to be polite."

"You're family, I don't need to be polite," Luke joked, leaning on his hand on the counter.

"Ha, ha."

"What do you want, C?"

"Well, I wanted to take my future sister-in-law shopping."

"Why?"

"So she could have some girl time before you lock her up in the tower," CindyLou joked.

"Whatever," he said, rolling his eyes and walking away.

"Oh, come on, we all know how much of an ogre you can be," she teased, walking over to him.

"Even with this baby face," she said, cutely, pinching his cheek.

He slapped her hand away, glaring at her.

"Even though you're giving me that look, I know you still love me," she picked.

"Whatever helps you sleep at night."

"At least, one of us is getting sleep," Kate joked.

Luke laughed as CindyLou started to gag and fake vomit. She looked over at Kate.

"Kate, I can't believe you're going to the dark side with him," CindyLou said, feigning shock.

"Well, he's my lone star in the night sky that guided me home," Kate said with a smile, looking over at Luke.

He walked over to her and placed his hand on her lower back as she wrapped her arms around his neck.

"I love you, too, babe," he said, before kissing her.

"Oh, God, you're making me feel sicker," CindyLou said. "I'll be in the car when you guys are done."

"It might take a while, or an hour," Kate teased, with a smirk on her face when Luke pulled away.

CindyLou shuddered and walked out. "Well, don't leave me out there too long or you'll have to throw me rations so I can survive out there."

Luke looked over at his sister. "What, you don't like this sweetness," he joked.

"Eeeew, no, especially with my baby brother." She looked at Kate. "Kate... boys are yucky by the way, they have cooties," she said, before leaving.

Luke and Kate laughed as they watched her leave, then turned their heads to look at each other.

"Now, where were we?" he asked, with a big smile.

"Us," she said softly.

"Oh, yeah," he whispered.

As he leaned in and kissed her slowly, her hands slid down and a slow, long groan escaped him as her fingers lightly touched his bare chest and then his abs. His chuckle became muffled when she covered his mouth with hers as she unbuckled his belt and undid his jeans again, picking up from when they were interrupted before. His hands gripped her hips and pulled her closer to him when she put him at her entrance. He slowly rocked against her as their sounds of pleasure were muffled by their mouths covered by each other's. A small smile snuck up on the corner of his mouth before it continued kissing Kate. His heart pounded from being so happy that he didn't really notice the dizziness. He didn't care, he had his girl.

Nothing will be able to take this away from me...

***

CindyLou pulled into a gas station with her convertible, while Kate sat in the passenger seat explaining to her about the ex from the other night. CindyLou just kept shaking her head.

"I still can't believe you stayed with him all those years."

"I know, I still can't either... I was really stupid."

"Oh, honey, you're not. Sometimes promises blind us and we can't see through the brightness until it becomes dim," CindyLou reassured her.

"Thanks, CindyLou."

"Please, call me C, like Luke does."

"Are you sure? I've never called you that before."

"Well, you're like family and you and Luke are the only family I have left," CindyLou said, with a smile.

Patting Kate's leg, CindyLou got out and started to work her gas tank to put gas in it.

"Now, let's stop worrying about the past and worry more about your wedding," CindyLou said, excitedly.

Kate laughed before staring into the distance. Biting her lower lip, she was pretty shaken up about talking about Mr. Wonderful, Dean Giuseppe. She couldn't believe how stupid she was to believe someone like that existed, but then realized that Mr. Wonderful did exist and his name was Luke. A smile slowly spread across her face as she realized how fate had intervened and brought her back to Luke.

"Hey," a male voice said.

Kate turned to see who had spoken, a punch to a face and couldn't see CindyLou standing by the car anymore. As she was about to get out of the car, still looking behind her, she felt a fistful of her hair being pulled. Her hands flew up to undo the tight grip, but before she knew it, she was up and out of the vehicle, struggling against being dragged, and immediately the violence.

"Bitch, did you really think you could leave me," Dean growled.

"Let me go!" Kate screamed.

"Fine," he grated.

Kate rolled on the ground as he tossed her like a rag doll, and watched in horror as a foot came toward her. She shielded her stomach with her arms to help protect the baby before his foot made contact. Curling into a ball, she made sure that she stayed conscious, as Dean continued to punch and kick her. She tried to cry out for help, but every time she moved to yell he punched her in the face.

***

Luke was whistling a happy tune, riding the tractor. He couldn't wipe the big smile off his face, as he felt like a new man. His whistling slowly faded when he heard his cellphone ringing with the annoying ringtone that CindyLou put on it. Looking at the screen, he could see a picture of him and his sister as she was being her usual embarrassing self by kissing his cheek with ruby red lipstick to leave a mark. His face was scrunched up from it as he tried pushing her away. Laughing, he slid to answer it, thinking she was calling to annoy him some more about how much better Kate was than him and wished Kate was her sister instead of him being her brother.

"Hey, ya can't go a few minutes without torturing me" he answered, stopping the tractor.

All he could hear was heavy breathing.

"C?" he questioned.

"Luke…"

"C, what's wrong?"

"Luke… it's him."

"Who?"

"It's Kate's ex… he's here."

Luke jumped off the tractor in a flash and started to walk fast. "Where are you?" he asked, sternly.

"Gerrity's Gas," she answered, between cries.

"I'm on my way," he snarled.

"Luke… don't…"

He hung up before she could tell him not to come and let the police handle it, but he had had enough of this guy. Running toward his vehicle, he jumped and slid across the hood of it before getting into the driver's side. He jammed the keys in, started it, and before it was completely ready, slammed on the gas pedal, causing it to shoot forward and speed away. He turned the steering wheel hard left, causing the car to drift sideways onto the main road. He could imagine his suspension and stuff was suffering, but he didn't care at this moment. The Charger let out a battle cry to let him know that it was ready for his combat with Kate's ex. As he raced his way to the gas station, he didn't care if a cop tried pulling him over, he wasn't going to stop until he laid his hands on the guy. Gripping the steering wheel tighter and clenching his jaw, he felt his blood boil as all he saw was red now. With ringing in his ears, he could hear the muffled sounds of Led Zepplin's *Immigrant Song* playing in the background. As they let out a yell on the radio, his car gave powerful roar as if from a mighty lion.

He almost drove by the gas station and turned his steering wheel hard to the right, causing the car to slid in the dirt and gravel. He slammed on the brakes as the car moaned and slid to a stop. He was out of the car in seconds and walking briskly over to where he saw a guy beating on Kate. Tapping him on his shoulder, the jerk turned around. Luke swung and punched him. He stared at Kate's ex and waited for him to get up. He was never going to fight a guy who was on the ground, no matter how angry he was. A wicked smile spread across his face when the idiot got up and charged at him. Luke slugged him again. Dean went down like a ton of bricks, and Luke watched as he struggled to get up.

"Stay down," Luke warned.

Even though he said it, he hoped the guy was a moron and would get up over and over again. He could beat the guy all day to let him know how wrong it was to hit a woman. Luke's smile grew when Dean got up again. He hit him with one punch and then another. He was easy with the first blow so he could hit the guy again before he fell to the ground. Looking over, he saw Kate laying there, just watching. He moved over toward her and as he helped her up, he saw she was beaten pretty bad.

"Are you okay?" he asked, quickly examining her.

Before she could answer, she looked over his shoulder.

"Luke, look out."

Luke turned in time to catch Dean's arm before he could punch him, and his fist made contact with Dean's gut. He folded over as Luke rolled his eyes at him for trying to sucker punch him. The guy still hadn't learned his lesson and kept trying to attack Luke, but he was able to avoid all the advances. He kept hitting him until he kicked the guy in the ass, causing him to run head first into a metal pole. Dean lay there for a moment, groaning then looked around and walked away. He felt Kate watching him, probably wondering what he was doing, but he had an idea as he spotted the jerk's black, Audi convertible.

***

Kate had no idea what Luke was doing, as he didn't seem tired from kicking Dean's ass, both literally and figuratively. Her eyes widened when she spotted Dean getting up, his face so twisted that she didn't even recognize him. His eyes burned right through her. Her body trembling, she was prepared to curl up in her ball as she had done so many times before.

"Fine, stay with your cowfucker, you whore," he snarled.

She flinched when he walked past her, unsure what he would do, but he continued to walk toward his car and climbed in it. Kate heard the rumbling sound of a big motor, and watched as a large dump truck backed up against the passenger side of Dean's car. Dean looked up in time to see the back tilt and dump its contents all over him and the car. Kate scrunched up her nose at the stench of the fresh manure. She watched as the pile moved a little to reveal a mouth coughing and vomiting up manure. Covering her face, she couldn't believe what had happened. Looking over, Luke walked toward her, but didn't seem like his happy-go-lucky self. He was sweating profusely, his face red as if he had run a marathon, hatred burning in his eyes, and she had to turn away from looking at him. Her body shook, having never seen him like this before, as she felt his hot breath against her skin, his breathing heavy.

"The grass was greener on that side, because it was fertilized with bullshit," he snarled.

Kate flinched when he stomped away.

"Fuck!" he shouted, leaving her where she stood.

***

Luke slid down the wall and closed his eyes to try to calm his heart. He had never felt such hatred for anyone, but when he saw what that asshole did to Kate, he completely lost it. Now, he was really suffering as his chest burned and his heart pounded so hard against his chest, he felt certain it would just pop out. His body shook as the sweat poured down his face. Smacking his lips together and swallowing hard, he felt so thirsty as his throat felt like sandpaper. He became worried that he might have set his illness in motion sooner rather than later.

"Luke?" CindyLou asked.

He waved her hand away as she tried to place it on him.

"Go check on Kate," he ordered, almost out of breath.

He listened as the dirt crunched under her shoes. He was glad she was listening to him as he wasn't able to fight with her right now. Tilting his head back, he felt the cool wall was nice compare to his head feeling as if it were on fire. The dizziness started to swarm worse as he had a moment to sit still. He heard the sirens in the distance, but that was all he heard before he passed out.

***

"I'm so sorry, CindyLou," Kate apologized.

CindyLou looked over at her, holding an ice pack to her face. "Don't worry about it, and please call me C."

"But we should have done something about him the other night," Kate stated.

"Hey, it's not your fault. It's the jerk's fault for sucker punching me. If he was man enough, he would have just head on punched me so I could show him how we country girls fight."

Kate couldn't help but laugh, but stopped when she held one of her ribs. The doctor told her she had some broken ribs, and having her arm in a cast didn't help. She was lucky that Luke showed up when he did or it could have been worse. Placing a hand on her stomach, she was glad she was able to protect the baby. She wouldn't know what to do if something happened to it. Looking around the waiting room, she wondered why they had to wait for so long for Luke. As far as she knew, he didn't have any injuries, but she didn't get a chance to see what happened to him after the manure incident. She was rushed in the ambulance as the techs were worried that she could have some internal injuries, but all the tests proved she didn't, so they released her. She found CindyLou after she was released, waiting in the waiting area of the emergency room. She looked around for Luke there, but CindyLou said he was being checked out. Something on her face was telling her that there was more to the story than him being checked out.

At that moment, the double swinging doors opened hard as a nurse and doctor chased after Luke.

"Sir, you need to stay," the doctor ordered.

"No, thanks, I'm good," Luke said, sliding a shirt on.

"But, sir, what about…" the doctor started.

Luke turned around. "Sorry, Doc, I'm leaving," he said, before turning around again.

"Luke?" Kate called out.

She wasn't sure if it would be her old Luke or the one she saw at the gas station. When she saw the smile and his eyes light up, she was relieved it was her old Luke. He hugged her tight until she flinched from her injuries. He quickly pulled away and examined her from top to bottom.

"I'm sorry, are you okay?"

"Yeah, some bumps and scrapes," she lied.

"Looks more than bumps and scrapes."

"I'm sorry," she said, looking sad.

"Hey, it's okay… some habits are hard to break."

"Luke, I'm so sorry about everything."

"Don't worry about it," he said, placing his hand on her stomach. "How's the baby?" he asked, nervously.

She placed her hand on his.. "The baby's fine. I did my best to protect it."

"Thank God," he sighed.

"Yes, most definitely," Kate whispered.

"I'm glad both of you are okay," he said, before kissing her gently.

"Both of you?" CindyLou asked, standing next to them.

Luke and Kate turned their heads to look at her with her eyes wide and her mouth hanging open.

"Is that why you're marrying her, because you knocked her up?" CindyLou accused.

"No," Luke said, sternly.

Kate laughed. "Trust me, C, I didn't know until after he proposed to me."

"Uh-huh, sure," she said, looking at Kate before smacking Luke.

"Ow, what was that for?" Luke whined.

"For keeping such great news like that from me," she said, crossly.

"C, no offense, but we weren't ready to spread the news yet until we were further along with it," Kate explained.

CindyLou nodded and then smacked Luke again.

"Ow, what was that one for?" he asked.

"For having me worry."

"Fine… can we get out of here now?" Luke asked.

He wrapped his arm around Kate's shoulders, looking around. Kate eyed him suspiciously as he seemed nervous.

"I hate hospitals," he muttered.

Kate was confused by the statement as most of his childhood he had been to the hospital many times for injuries and broken bones, but she had never heard him say that before. Before she could ask him, he looked at her with a smile to hid the nervousness that still showed on his face.

"So, babe, want to go out somewhere special tonight?" he asked.

Kate didn't know how to answer him as they had just been through the hellish ordeal.

"Are you sure that's wise?"

"Yeah." Shrugging his shoulders. "Somewhere out of town to clear our heads of this mess."

"Um, okay," she answered, unsure.

"I'm with Kate, are you sure that's wise?" CindyLou questioned, arching her eyebrow.

Luke looked over at her. "Yeah, and don't worry, I'll have my phone on me the whole time."

CindyLou rolled her eyes and let out a heavy sigh before walking ahead of them and leaving them behind. Kate just looked at her, not sure what was wrong.

"What's she mad about?" Kate asked.

"Nothing, just being a nervous nelly," Luke joked, nervously.

"You're not hiding anything from me are you?"

"No... No, babe, I wouldn't."

"Okay, remember we promised each other that we wouldn't hide anything from each other anymore."

***

He pulled her tighter against him. "I know, babe... I know," he said softly.

They continued their walk in silence, Luke chewing on his lower lip as his stomach twisted. He felt sure Kate had figure out that he was hiding something, but she seemed to drop it. He didn't need her to worry until after they had completed more of his bucket list, then he would tell her everything.

Soon, babe... Soon...

***

Luke kept moving items on the table, nervous about being in a fancy restaurant. He had never done this with Kate before as they were always satisfied with a greasy burger at an In/Out diner. He stopped fidgeting when she placed her hand on top of his and looked up quickly before laughing nervously. His leg started to shake as he couldn't sit still and his heart pounded harder and harder each second that went by. Kate turned his hand over to hold it, but heat hit his face when he realized his hand was sweaty. He quickly dried it and placed it back for Kate to hold. He looked across the table and saw how elegant she looked in a new olive-colored dress that was snugged against her curves. Her hair was professionally done up and she wore jewelry that he just purchased for her. Kate looked beyond beautiful as she shimmered in the dim light. As he stretched out his arm, his sleeve revealed a Rolex watch she had purchased for him. They really looked the part of belonging in the big city's restaurant.

He had never really done anything like this before as he always looked like a small town country boy. The only time he dressed up for an event was when he had to attend a wedding or a funeral. His agent wanted them to meet at fancy places like this, but he always rejected the invite because he hated being dressed like this. It wasn't him and he didn't feel comfortable in his skin when he wore a monkey suit. He kept playing with his tie as it felt as if it were strangling him.

"You know, we didn't need to eat out like this," Kate whispered, across the table.

"I know, I just wanted to treat you."

Even when she rolled her eyes, he knew if she was really the kind of girl who dressed the way she was, she would never give him a second of her time. Lucky for him, it was Kate who was sitting across from him. She seemed to be more comfortable dressed like this, but then he recalled how she told him she was arm candy for the jerk, so she probably had to act and dress a certain way. He leaned over the table so she could hear him.

"Are you okay?"

"Yeah, I'm fine, just a little achy."

"Good, but I meant the way you're dressed and all."

A big smile appeared on her face. "Luke, I'm with you, it doesn't matter how I'm dressed or where I am, just as long as I'm with you."

Smiling, he sat back, happy to hear her answer. Before they could carry on their conversation, he looked to his side when he heard squealing.

"Oh my God, it's you!" one girl screamed.

"I can't believe, you're really here," another one squealed.

"Oh, my God, I love all your songs," a third chimed in.

Luke looked over at Kate who was giggling, trying to hide it with her hand. He looked back at the girls who were apparently here with their parents.

"I'm glad you guys enjoy my music, but I'm here on a private matter."

"Ohhhh," the three girls whined, pouting.

"Luke, don't be rude to your fans," Kate teased.

He looked over and saw a smirk on her face. Laughing, he turned toward the girls.

"Okay, okay, I'm sorry," he said, with a big smile.

"Oh, thank you, thank you, thank you," one girl chanted.

Luke took the notepad from the girl. "What's your name, sweetie?"

"Oh, my God, he called me sweetie," she squealed, trying to hide the redness on her cheeks.

He just looked at her, waiting for her to calm down.

"Oh, it's Allison."

"Allison... here you go."

The second girl handed him a CD that he showed to Kate. He could see she was enjoying this as her smirk got bigger as she tried not to laugh.

"And what's your name, darling?" he asked.

"Jenna," she answered, trying to hold in her excitement.

"Here you go, and who's next."

"Amber," the last girl answered, quickly.

"Alright, here you go, Amber," he wrote her name and signed a cowboy hat.

"Oh, Mister Jackson, could we have a quick picture?" Jenna asked.

"Well, I don't know..." he started.

"Yeah, why not, cowboy?" Kate teased.

Before he could reply to her, she stood and took the camera from Jenna.

"Here, let me take a pic of you guys," she said.

The girls squealed and giggled, as Kate looked from behind the camera.

"Come on, Luke, don't keep your fans waiting," she joked.

Luke laughed as he stood and took his spot between the girls. They all squeezed close to him. A flash went off and Luke was about to sit down again.

"Oh no, country boy, you need to have more than one pic," Kate said, smiling broadly.

Luke rolled his eyes as he knew she was enjoying his torture. He wasn't big on pictures unless it was with Kate. After what felt like an eternity, Kate finally had her fill of fun and handed the camera back to Jenna.

"Thank you so much, miss," Jenna said, excitedly.

"No problem, kid," she answered, with a smile.

"Who are you?" Amber asked.

"Well, ladies, you're in luck, that would be my fiancée and the muse for my music," Luke answered.

Before Kate knew it, the girls had all gathered around her and were touching her as if she were a unicorn. Kate glared over at Luke as he continued to laugh. The girls began to ask for selfies with Kate, so she took their cellphones and posed with them, made silly faces, and had fun doing selfies with the girls. Luke laughed harder as she was more popular than he was as the girls wanted to hear stories and wanted her autograph too. After a while, the girls finally left and Luke was able to have his Kate back.

"So, what do you think about becoming a country singer?" Luke teased.

"It would be fun to do someday."

"So, you don't want to go on tour with me?"

"Not at the moment, as we have so much going on right now. Maybe after the little one is born."

"Okay."

He watched as Kate looked at her menu. So many thoughts roamed his mind and his stomach knotted further as a nagging message from his sister kept pestering him, but he ignored it, not wanting to ruin the moment.

So, when are you going to tell her, Luke?

-C

***

Luke stood at the hotel's window, staring at the city lights. His cellphone kept buzzing all night and he couldn't sleep, as his sister kept reminding him of his troubling issue. He looked down at the fiftieth message from her.

Luke, please don't do this to her. Please think this through.

He watched as another message lit up the screen.

You should come home. I'm worried what might happen while you're away like the last time...

He tried to break his phone in half from the annoyance of his sister being right, eventually throwing it against the wall, then froze and watched as Kate stirred in bed. Exhaling slowly, he was glad she was still asleep. He didn't need her to worry about his medical condition right now and looked once more out the window. He had the opportunity to move to the big city, but realized it wasn't for him, plus his condition wouldn't allow him. Moving toward the bed, he crawled back in and pulled Kate closer to him. Sighing with content, he was happy at least to have her back in his life.

***

"Now, if anyone has any objections as to why these two shouldn't be marry, please speak now or forever hold your peace," the justice of the peace said.

"None of you better open your damn mouths or I'll kick your ass," CindyLou warned.

Kate and Luke laughed as they could imagine CindyLou standing behind them and looking around. After the justice of the peace had a good chuckle, he looked back at Kate and Luke.

"I now pronounce you man and wife. You may kiss the bride."

As Luke kissed Kate, there was cheering and hollering from the small crowd they had invited to witness their wedding.

They turned to face the group and *My Light* by Sully Erna started to play as they walked down the aisle. People blew bubbles toward them as they moved past them.

***

At the end of the reception, it was just Kate and Luke swaying to the music playing on the nearby stereo. He nuzzled against the nape of her neck as she rested her head on his shoulder.

"Mmmm, not a bad CD," she said, quietly.

"Thank you, I wasn't sure how good it would be."

"Well, you're a good singer."

"So, are you."

"I know," she teased.

He chuckled. "Babe, you're so fucking awesome."

"I know."

After laughing again, he trailed kisses along her jawline. "So, modest," he teased, quietly.

"Not so much, seeing as I've been inside your pants the whole time you were talking."

Luke knew she was right as he was too busy enjoying her this close to him that he didn't realize she had undone his belt and pants and had a hand inside, stroking him. Pulling away from her, he could see lust in her eyes.

"Did you want this, Mrs. Jackson?" he said, huskily, his hand on top of hers in his pants.

"I thought you would never ask, Mr. Jackson," she said, seductively.

Placing his mouth on hers, he hungrily kissed her to show how much he needed her. His hands found her butt cheeks and squeezed them, causing her to jolt toward him. He picked her up as she wrapped her legs around him. He moved them toward the Charger, laid her back on the hood, and pulled her butt toward the edge as she spread out over the hood.

"Oh, God, babe, you always look fucking sexy on this car.".

"Well, don't waste your time just staring at me."

"Impatient?"

"I love feeling your cock inside me."

"Oh, babe, if you keep talking like that, it gets me so turned on that I might blow right here, right now."

"I want to feel it inside me."

"Yes, darling," he said, in his southern drawl.

His arms slid under her legs as she rested her heels on his back and he began to rock into her.

"Fuck, babe, you always feel incredible," he said, through his clenched jaw.

"Shut up and fuck me, cowboy," she moaned.

"I love it when you talk like that. It makes me so much harder in you."

"Oh, yeah, I'll keep talking if you keep saying things like that."

"You feel that, babe, that's *all* for you."

"Ohhh, give it to me, Luke."

"Oh, God, babe, I'm like going balls deep."

"If you like that, then you're going to love these."

She unbuttoned the top of her spring dress and unclasped her bra, revealing her breasts to him.

"Mmm, yes I do... you have fucking fantastic tits."

"You're slowing down, cowboy," she teased.

"I'm sorry, darling," he said, back in his southern drawl.

As he thrust harder and faster into her, he watched her breasts bounce with the rhythm of their lovemaking and her moans turned to screams of pleasure that echoed in the empty area. The only thing that responded were the cattle in the distance. The moonlight spotlighted her on the hood of the car that gave a glimmering aura around her. If he didn't know any better, he would say she was an angel... his angel.

Leaning over, he held her close as he had so much happiness in his heart that was ready to explode. He had his girl, he married her and soon would have a family with her. Life couldn't be any better.

As she clenched onto him, he felt her convulse under him as he bucked a few times in her. As the air escaped his body, he was beyond exhausted, but exhilarated at the same time. The moment was amazing and he couldn't dream of not being with the woman he loved. She slowly brushed her fingers through his hair as he tried to calm down his heart so his symptoms would go away. He didn't need to worry her by passing out again.

"I love you, Luke," she whispered.

"Ditto," he teased back, quietly.

***

Sneaking out of the bedroom, Luke crept across the hall to the bathroom. He slowly shut the door and walked over the corner of the bathroom before kneeling on one knee. Popping up the floorboard, he took out a medication bottle that had all his information and the name of the medication on it: *Metoprolol.* He took one pill, put the bottle back in, and replaced the floorboard. He filled the glass a quarter full and popped the pill in his mouth before drinking the water. Once done, he placed the glass on the counter and went to leave the bathroom. He jumped back with his hand over his heart as Kate scared him.

"I'm sorry, didn't mean to scare you. I thought you were taking a shower without me."

"It's okay," Luke said, before giving a wink. "I would never take a shower without you ever again," he joked, before pulling her tight against him so he could kiss her.

Thinking to himself, it was ironic that he just took medication to slow his heart rate and Kate just caused it to go into overdrive.

***

As they got closer to the barn, Luke put his arm out to stop Kate from going any farther.

"What's wrong?" Kate asked.

"Do you hear that?"

At that moment, they heard the sound of rushing water. Luke ran before Kate could say anything else.

106

"Damn it!" she heard him say from the barn.

Jogging in, she could see a big hose that was taped down and punctured, spraying water all over the nicely stacked hay.

"No… No, no, no," Luke chanted, angrily, gripping his head after throwing down his cowboy hat.

Kate's eyes wandered over the hay and couldn't believe someone would do this. She knew it wasn't an accident as it was apparent that someone took the time to tape down the huge hose and puncture it just right to spray over all the hay that was meant for the cattle. Placing her hand on his shoulder, she could see how disheartened he was. She could imagine that it must have taken him a while to get this all set up, seeing as she never saw another soul around here helping him.

"It'll be okay, Luke," she reassured him.

"How?" he asked, sadly.

"We'll get through this like everything else, trust me," she said, with a smile.

Wrapping her in his arms, he held her tightly against him. She could sense something coming from him, but couldn't put her finger on it. She inhaled his musk and just enjoyed being like this with him.

"I'm so glad to have you back, Kate," he whispered.

"Me, too," she said quietly, closing her eyes.

Her eyes slowly opened when she felt his body shaking. She wondered what was wrong, but he tightened his hold on her to where she just stayed nuzzled and snugged against him.

***

Kate was helping Luke to get rid of the wet hay by loading it on a trailer, but started to worry about him as he moved slowly. She offered to carry the hay from the spot to the trailer, but he refused her. He told her that she should be taking it easy after the beating and being pregnant. Kate just rolled her eyes at him as he was being ridiculous, but she started to wonder if there was something else going on as he leaned up against a pole and removed his cowboy hat to wipe his brow, closing his eyes.

"Hey, are you okay?" she asked.

"Yeah," he quickly answered, eyes still closed and the back of his hand on his forehead.

She didn't like the uneasiness around them.

"Don't tell me you're getting slow in your old age?" she teased.

Soon a smile appeared on his face as he looked at her. She was happy to see his smile return. Hoping off the trailer, she slowly walked over to him and placed her hands on his chest.

"Hey, I have a surprise for you."

"Another one?" he questioned, arching his eyebrow.

"Of course, cowboy," she teased, as she tugged on his hand to follow.

As they rounded into another area of the large barn, she held up her arms to show him the area.

"Tada," she announced.

***

Luke took a few more steps in and looked around in amazement before looking back at her.

"What's this?" he asked.

"Well, I recalled how much you wanted to travel the world when we were younger and I imagine you didn't get a chance to, so I set this up," she explained.

Looking back at the area, Kate had set up different stations with different decorations, food, and drinks from all over the world. Shaking his head, he couldn't believe she had done all of this.

"So, don't tell me you already did this?"

"Nah, babe, I'm just still shocked that you did this."

Wrapping her arms around his. "You've done so much for me, Luke, I wanted to return the favor."

"You didn't have to, babe. I love you and wanted to do it."

"I know. Ditto," she teased.

He took off his cowboy hat and placed it on her head. "You're fucking amazing, babe," he said, before planting a kiss on her lips.

Cupping her face, he wanted to keep kissing her, but she pushed him away with her hands on his chest.

"Come on, cowboy, we can do that later," she teased.

"Okay, let's see what we have here," he said, turning to look at everything.

He didn't know where to start as everything looked good. Moving toward the Ireland station first, he examined what looked like pancakes, but with different coloration. He picked one up and took a bite, nodding his approval.

"Those are potato pancakes," she explained.

He moved on to Scotland and eyed the collection of what looked like scrapple put into a giant hotdog casing with suspicion. Cautiously, he cut into it and took a bit and chewed it for a while.

"Wow, despite looking weird, it tastes pretty good," he complimented.

"That would be haggis," she said, with a smirk.

"What is it?"

"Sheep stomach filled with meat," she answered quickly, her smile becoming bigger.

Luke quickly spit out the second helping that was in his mouth and looked over at Kate as she laughed.

"Are you trying to kill me, because, babe, you already have everything of mine?" he questioned.

"But not your soul," she said, and laughed evilly, rubbing her hands together.

Shaking his head, he was about to say something, but he noticed something. Looking over her, he saw smoke coming from the area they were in. His eyes widened as he quickly picked up Kate and ran out of the barn.

As he put her back on her feet, she looked behind him. He turned to watch as flames shot out of all the openings. He could see through the doorway they came out of was filled with heavy smoke. Then he felt her hand on his arm.

"Luke, my notebook."

"What?"

"I left my notebook in there."

Before she could stop him, he jolted to a run and shot into the barn and started coughing as he used one arm to shield his eyes as he found his way around inside, so concerned about her notebook that he had forgotten about his safety. He knew people would think he was stupid to go back for it, but it was the only thing she was going to have left after he… A beam fell in front of him with a loud crash, and he looked around, trying to figure out how to get past it.

***

Kate couldn't believe that Luke ran back in there. She didn't know why she thought of her notebook as she watched the flames take over the barn. She could see the heavy smoke fuming out of it as she realized that the wet hay was causing it to be smokier. She paced around as she tried to figure out what to do. A loud crash caused her to stop and stare in horror at the barn as the roof collapsed.

"Luke!" she screamed.

As she was about to run in after him, she watched a figure stumble out of it. Luke collapsed on his hands and knees, coughing, and she ran over and knelt next him. She examined him and could see that he was just covered in sod, so happy he was okay. He lifted his hand and she saw he was gripping the notebook so hard that his knuckles were white. Before she could grab the notebook, he collapsed on his side. Kate's eyes widened as she tried to wake Luke and checked his pulse, glad to find he still had one, but it was racing like crazy. As she shook harder, she realized he was unconscious. Pulling out her phone, she dialed for help.

"Yes, please help me… my husband," she began.

CHAPTER EIGHT

Kate listened as the cop explained to her that the fire at the barn was caused by arson. Kate's body began to shake as she realized who was doing it. Especially, with the hose incident. She began to worry about Luke's safety as she was trying to decide what would be best. His safety or her heart. Before she could decide, a doctor walked up to her.

"Kate... you can see him now," the doctor said.

Kate didn't waste any time as she rushed to Luke's room. Tears streamed down her face as she knew he almost died. She was told he suffered smoke inhalation, after that she didn't hear what else she was told as so many thoughts rushed through her mind.

"Oh, Luke," she cried to herself.

As she rounded the corner and entered his room, she saw Luke talking to Johnboy.

"Are you sure about this?" Johnboy asked.

"It's for the best... C was right, I shouldn't have done this to her," Luke said, sadly.

"Did what?" Kate asked.

Johnboy and Luke looked at her.

"Well, that's my cue to leave," Johnboy said, quickly exiting the room.

Kate watched as he left before looking back at Luke.

"Kate," he said, with a raspy voice.

"Oh, Luke, I'm so glad you're okay," she said, before rushing to the side of the bed.

She tried to hug him, but he stopped her and placed her hands back against her with his one hand. She began to shake more as she didn't like the look on his face. It was as if someone had just run over his dog.

"Kate… I have something to tell you," Luke said, slowly.

"What is it, Luke?" she asked, with panic in her voice.

"Katelyn…"

She could tell this was something hard for him to say as he didn't really call her by her full name and he was struggling with something, as his eyes revealed an internal turmoil. His eyes finally locked onto hers.

"Katelyn, I lied to you."

"About what?"

"About that I didn't have any more secrets."

"What do you mean?"

"I didn't tell you the real reason why I wanted you to come home with me."

"Luke, you're not making any sense."

"The real reason I wanted you to be with me for this second chance was so I didn't die alone."

Kate just stared at him as if he had lost his mind.

"Luke, you're still not well, let me see if I can get you something," she said, trying to walk away, but Luke grabbed hold of her hand.

"Of course, I'm not well… Remember that bull that kicked me in the chest years ago?"

"Yeah…" she said, unsure.

"Well, apparently, it did more damage than I thought… Kate, my heart is damaged and I don't have long to live."

"What?" she cried, tears flowing down her face.

"I found out how much damage I had when I was on tour and passed out. The exact same thing happened that one night when I passed out with you."

Kate just stared at him in disbelief. He could tell the wheels were turning as she recalled the night he passed out on her.

He held up a folded piece of yellow paper. "This is my bucket list… I'm so sorry, but I wanted to die in your arms."

She slowly took the paper and unfolded it. Clenching her jaw, she felt the anger flowing through her as her tears hit the paper. She read each thing on the list and saw that some were crossed out. Looking back at him, she now understood why they were doing these things. She just thought he was just going through some early mid-life crisis, but this whole time he was just using her so he could die happy. Crumpling the paper, she threw it at him.

"How dare you?" she questioned, angrily.

"I'm so sorry, Kate… I didn't mean to hurt you," he pleaded.

"Well, you did," she said, fisting her hands.

Turning his head away from her. "That's why I don't want you around me anymore…you were just a phase… I realized I don't really love you," he said, slowly.

"Fuck you, Luke," she said, angrily.

***

He swallowed hard as he listened to her walk out of his room. Screwing his eyes shut, the tears escaped. He clenched his jaw to keep from letting out cries. He didn't want her to second guess his words. His body shaking, his heart was broken to a million pieces as he let her go. It was a hard decision, but he knew he had to do it or she would be hurt even more. Just before she came in, Johnboy and he were going over some of his affairs and that was when he told Johnboy what he was going to do. Even Johnboy didn't believe him at first, but eventually, being his lawyer, he accepted what he said. After he was gone, Kate would get everything as

Luke had changed his will with Johnboy minutes before Kate showed up. She could do whatever she wanted with all his assets and millions in the bank account, just as long as she was happy and wasn't sad about his passing.

He started to cough as the sobs in his chest were too much. He had to sit up to cough and sob. Spotting the crumpled up paper, he threw it as hard as he could across the room before crashing back on his back. He stared up at the ceiling, wishing he had never seen her at the gas station. He should have just gotten into his car and driven away.

"I'm such an asshole," he whispered to himself.

***

Kate looked around the room to make sure she wasn't missing anything. Lucky for her, Luke was still at the hospital as they needed to keep an eye on him due to the smoke inhalation. As she slowly placed the last of her clothing in a bag, she realized it was almost like the time before, but this time she wasn't rushing. She was dragging her feet as her heart didn't want her to leave, but her mind had made its decision. She couldn't stay here as she knew she would have the painful reminder about Luke. Even if she stayed, he would only survive so long and then he'd be gone. She couldn't go through that pain.

Zipping up her bag, she took one more look around before wrapping an arm around herself. She felt a chill as the room seemed so uninviting. Deciding to leave now, she rushed out of the house and hopped in the cab that was waiting for her.

"Where to, miss?" the cab driver asked.

"Bus depot, please."

As he drove away, she looked out the window, watching as the world she knew disappeared behind her. The last time she did this, it wasn't as heart wrenching as Luke drove her to the bus depot, as the bus drove away, he didn't look back when he walked away. Her heart had dropped, thinking he was going to stop her, but he didn't. He let her go…

***

Johnboy carried a bag as Luke held onto his chest and dragged himself toward Johnboy's car.

"Take me to Mick's," Luke ordered.

"Shouldn't you go home and rest?"

"That wasn't a request."

"Luke, I don't think…"

"I didn't ask for your thoughts, besides there's just bad memories at home," Luke said, sadly, with a sigh.

***

Kate stared out the bus window, letting out a sigh, as memories of Luke swarmed her mind and she felt the tears threatening to fall. As the bus kept going, Kate saw a sign:

Home is where the Heart is.

Kate didn't think much about it until she saw another sign with a heart on it:

Giving life is like giving love… Be a donor today…

Kate started to feel strange as she kept reading signs about love and where she should be. Then she began to hear a song play on the bus' radio. Now, she believed she was getting hints from someone as *Let Me Go* by Avril Lavigne played.

"This is crazy, it's not as if a sign is going to tell me to go back," she whispered to herself.

Then she saw it, a construction sign flashes: *Turn around now*

Kate couldn't believe her eyes. If she didn't know any better, she would say someone was really trying to tell her what to do. The song, *Closer* by The Chainsmokers popped on the radio. Kate remembered singing this song with Luke when she came back into town. There was static and another song, *Small Town Boy* by Dustin Lynch began playing.

Her phone buzzed as she received a message. Looking at the screen, she saw the background picture of her and Luke. A teardrop hit the screen as she could see how happy they were. She searched for the message and spotted a photo from one of the girls they had met at the restaurant when she was with Luke. Without warning, her phone became possessed as so many pictures of Luke suddenly flash across her phone, ones where he was making funny faces at her or where she caught him with his shirt off and wearing his cowboy hat. Kate tried to get rid of the pictures, but more kept popping up. She must have accidently hit something as her Pandora app popped opened and first played *Pieces* by Red and then it went to country and played his song about her leaving him.

One day you got up and left me behind

I wished you'd asked if I mind

Sweet, sweet Katelyn

Where have you been

I hope you found greener pastures

As I moped like a bastard

Kate just stared at the screen, her mind frozen, shocked by what was happening. She knew what she had to do as she threw her phone into the bag next to her so she could ignore it. It continued to buzz, but she continued to ignore it as she looked out the window anxiously.

***

Luke chugged his beer quickly and slammed the mug down.

"Another," he ordered, exhaling sharply.

"Hey, man, don't you think you had enough?" Mick asked.

"I'll tell you when I've had enough. Now, I would like another," he ordered.

"I don't think this is helping your heart," Mick questioned.

"Well, nothing else is going to fix it…unless you believe duct tape could." Luke just glared at Mick as he stood up and went to get him another drink. "Didn't think so," he muttered under his breath.

The jukebox jolted alive and started to play the song *Let Her Go* by Passengers. As Luke listened to the song, he screwed his eyes shut, trying to keep from breaking down. Whatever he had left of his heart, was breaking into a million pieces. Swallowing hard, he tried to figure what he was going to do now.

After the song ended, *She's All I Ever Need* by Ricky Martin starting playing. Luke tried covering his ears, but the song was able to penetrate and play in his head. Covering his head, he fisted his hair desperate for this madness to stop. It was hard the first time and he knew it was going to be much harder this time.

Then, *Things Left Unsaid* by Disciple began. Clenching his jaw, he couldn't deal with this shit now and it wasn't helping.

"Mick, what the hell is wrong with the jukebox?" Luke questioned, angrily.

Not really hearing a response, Luke tried to tune out the song, but each lyric was a stab into his heart. His body shook as he tried his best to keep from breaking down. As the song ended, a teardrop slowly slid down his face until it hit the counter. He could hear a door swinging open and some muffled voices, but ignored them as he wanted to be left alone. He exhaled sharply when someone finally unplugged the jukebox. Listening, he heard someone place a guitar case on the stage and move around. A stool scraped across the stage floor.

"Hi ya, I'm here to sing a song to a very special cowboy," a female announced.

Luke slowly opened his eyes. He wasn't sure if he was hearing correctly, but the female voice sounded a lot like Kate. As he listened to the strumming of the guitar, he gradually looked over at the stage and saw what he thought was an illusion. Sitting on the stage was Kate playing his guitar.

***

Kate cleared her throat again as she kept playing the chords on his guitar. She had never done anything like this without Luke by her side. She only sang in front of him and now she was singing in front of a group of regulars as well. Swallowing hard, she knew how she wanted the song to go as she came up with some of the lyrics the one morning when she was strumming on the guitar, humming, and the rest came to her as she ran all the way here. Looking over at Luke, she could see how much it hurt him to let her go again. He was disheveled and scruffy looking. Once they locked eyes, she began to sing.

You are my lone star

You are what you are

In the night sky

You are my guide

To be home with you

Because of you

I am who I am

And I am glad

You're my life

I'm your wife

I was searching for my north star

Never thought it would be right in front of me

I went the other way

Led along like a wide-eyed puppy

I thought I found what I wanted but

He wasn't what I thought he was

***

As Kate kept singing, Luke found it hard to believe she was here and singing to him. Not in the Charger, not at home, but in front of other people. Even though she wanted to be a country singer, she always became anxious when singing in front of others and that's why it worked when they both were together as she felt confident and safe by his side.

He slowly staggered toward the stage, keeping his eyes locked with Kate. He was still in awe of her being here as he believed he was going to wake up in the hospital and it was all a dream.

You're the lone star

In my night sky

You're my guide

You had every chance to set me free

But I keep coming back

So bring me home tonight

Bring me home tonight...

Luke stopped right in front of her, never moving his eyes as she finished the song.

"So, what do you say, cowboy," she asked.

***

Kate bit her lower lip as her stomach twisted. Luke didn't move or say a word, he just stared at her. She became twitchy on the stool, hating the awkward silence.

"Can you at least say something?" she begged.

Looking away, she realized she was imagining everything that was sending her back here. As she got off the stool, she slid off the strap and placed the guitar back in its case.

"I guess I was just crazy," she muttered to herself.

As she turned around, she was surprised as Luke held her face between his hands and slammed his lips on hers. She wasn't expecting this, as he didn't seem to care that she had come back, but apparently she was wrong. She was still in the moment when he pulled away and held her tight against him.

"Please, don't ever leave me, again, babe," he pleaded.

Wrapping her arms around him. "I promise," she whispered a vow in his ear.

***

Kate waddled down the steps with Luke's help, rubbing her swollen stomach a few times.

"Are you okay," Luke asked, nervously.

"Yeah, just a rowdy kid today," she joked.

"I would say, seeing as it has this one's genes," CindyLou teased, poking Luke in the shoulder.

"You do realize that it wasn't just me getting in trouble, Kate was there," Luke explained.

"Whatever, baby brother, you should know you're going to be blamed for everything," CindyLou said, rolling her eyes.

"And why are you coming along?" Luke asked.

"Well, Kate needs all the moral support she can get seeing as it won't come from you, dick," CindyLou explained.

"I apologized a million times to her for my actions, plus that was a few months ago."

"Well, it was so hurtful it stained."

"Alright, kids, if we can't behave, I'm going on my own," Kate said, pushing past both of them toward the car.

"See what you did?" CindyLou said sternly.

"What I did… how about you?"

"Uh-huh, we Jackson women stick together."

"Great, well I'm hoping for a boy then."

"I'm hoping for a girl so it'll be three against one," CindyLou teased.

As Luke rolled his eyes, CindyLou smiled at her victory.

"Maybe three against two, little bro," she muttered to herself.

***

"So, do you guys want to know the sex of your baby," the tech asked.

Luke rubbed Kate's hand between his as she nodded. After they made up, like a million times the day she came back, they had a long discussion about their future. It was a discussion he didn't really want to have, but he knew Kate needed to know what to expect. They even took a drive over to Johnboy's office so they could go through the important documents and affairs. It took some time, but Kate eventually felt at ease with him again.

Now, they were at the doctor's office, seeing how their little one was doing. As the tech moved the wand around, Luke watched with awe at how a little human could grow inside Kate. Eventually, the tech stopped the wand and smiled.

"Well, I like to announce that you're going to have a girl," the tech said, excitedly.

Luke couldn't help but laugh as his sister was right. Even though the baby was going to be a girl, he didn't mind, as all he hoped was that his child would grow to be happy and healthy.

***

"Come to think of it, cowboy, you never let me drive the Charger," Kate stated.

"Well, that's because you were doing other things," Luke teased, with a wink.

"Oh, God, I think I'm going to vomit," CindyLou said, rolling her eyes.

Luke laughed before tossing the keys to Kate. He opened the passenger's door and pulled up the front seat for CindyLou to get in.

"Uh, no, little bro, I'm sitting in the front with the Jackson women," CindyLou ordered with a little shove toward him.

"Fine," Luke said.

He sat in the middle of the back seat as the girls got in, his arms spread across the back of his seat as tried to get comfortable.

"Feels so lonely back here," he teased, winking at Kate when she looked up at the rearview mirror.

Kate giggled before starting up the car and placing a hand on the dashboard.

"I love how this car purrs," she said.

"Well, if you like purring, I could do something with your pussy," Luke joked.

"Oh my God, Luke, enough. I would like to keep my stomach,"

CindyLou yelled.

Kate and Luke both laughed before Kate pulled out of the parking lot.

***

Luke had his head tilted back with the cowboy hat covering his face as the girls upfront were singing with the radio. Kate stopped at the intersection as a memory of her playing her game with Luke when he took her out shopping popped in her head. It made her hot and bothered as she looked up in the rearview mirror to see him sleeping in the back. He was awake most of the night as she had bad aches and false labor as it was too early for the baby to come out yet. So she made sure to let him sleep as her and his sister enjoyed some girl time. She decided they would go out to eat and turned off her left turn signal. She double checked the intersection before pulling out. Even though they were all stops, she wanted to be careful with Luke's car. She and CindyLou were laughing about something when, without warning, a black BMW smashed right into the driver's side of the Charger. The car went flying, hit the ground on its roof, and rolled a few times before sliding to a stop.

Luke tried to move, but he was strapped in tightly against the seat. He looked at Kate and CindyLou in the front and saw they were unconscious. Eventually, his vision became blurry as something wet pooled in his eye and he began to get tunnel vision before passing out. He could hear his heart pounding in his ears as the dizziness swarmed.

***

Luke woke up to find ceiling lights zoom above him. He groaned, trying to move, but someone kept him on the stretcher. He tried removing the oxygen mask to talk, but someone just put it back on. Looking around, he spotted a lot of medical people, all talking at once. He wanted to know what happened to Kate and CindyLou.

He felt a jerk as he was placed in a bay. Looking over to his right, he spotted Kate being rolled in. He let out another groan when he noticed she was still unconscious and looked really bad. Looking over at another bay, he saw CindyLou being brought in with bandages on one leg and arm soaked through with blood. She too was unconscious. When he saw another stretcher roll into another bay, Luke tried to jerk against the restraints on him. He so wanted to murder the person on the stretcher.

"You son of a bitch… I'm going to fucking kill you!" Luke yelled, through the oxygen mask.

A couple of people pushed him back on the stretcher and restrained him so they could take care of him. Luke kept glaring at Dean Giuseppe. He wished he could just go over there and kill the guy then come back to be checked out. He should have known that a psychopath like Dean wasn't going to let things go. As they closed the curtain around Dean, Luke looked up at the ceiling, as he felt so many emotions rushing through him. Tears streamed down his face as he tried to grasp what had happened.

A panic alarm beeping got his attention. As he looked over at Kate, he could see medics rushing around as her heart rate dropped. Luke tried to get off the stretcher again, but his monitor beeped constantly as his heart raced more. Soon, he felt the dizziness before he fell against the stretcher after passing out.

***

Well, I wished I could say everything worked out. That my daughter and Kate were running around with the family dog. CindyLou was torturing me as usual as I cooked up some burgers on the grill, but unfortunately, life is unfair and fate can be both kind and cruel.

***

Luke slowly opened his eyes and his hand went to his chest. It felt as if his chest had been ripped open and sewn back together.

"Hey, bud," Johnboy said, with a smile.

"Johnboy?"

"How are you feeling?"

"Like shit."

"I can only imagine after having a heart transplant."

"What?" Luke gasped, confusion in his voice.

"Wow, man, take it easy, you've been out for a while and just had heart surgery."

"I don't understand… How did I get a heart?"

"Well, they found a donor for you."

"But I was on the bottom of the list."

"Well, this one was a special request."

Luke looked around at his hospital room.

"Where's Kate?" he asked, groggily.

"Well…" Johnboy started.

Luke quickly looked over at him.

"Johnboy, where's Kate?" Luke asked again.

"Luke, I don't know how to say this without breaking lawyer-client confidentiality."

Tears ran down Luke's face. "Oh no… Please… Please, don't tell me… the heart…" Luke choked out between sobs.

"I'm sorry, man," Johnboy said, looking at the ground.

Luke looked over and saw someone had left behind a stethoscope.

"Give me that," he asked, sadly.

"The stethoscope?"

"Yes, damn it."

"Okay… Okay."

Luke practically ripped the instrument out of Johnboy's hand, quickly put the earpieces in his ears, and moved the hospital gown to reveal his bare chest. He ignored the coldness of the stethoscope as he needed to know. Closing his eyes, he took some calming breaths. As he slowly opened his eyes, tears streamed down his face. He listened to the heart beat in his chest. *Kate's* heartbeat.

As he leaned over, he began to sob harder. "No… No, it can't be true," Luke choked out.

Throwing the stethoscope across the room, not believing what had happened.

"Goddammit!" he yelled, before covering his face as he sobbed harder.

***

Standing at a big window, he looked in, holding onto his IV pole. He had sneaked down to see how his baby girl was doing. According to Johnboy, they had to do an emergency C-section to remove her before Kate went for surgery for her injuries. The baby was premature, so it had to stay in the NICU. Luke couldn't remove his eyes from the precious life inside the plastic-walled fortress protecting her from the outside world. Luke wished he could have done the same for Kate. If only he didn't let her drive, then she would be here. It wasn't as if he had long to live, but apparently Kate had talked to Johnboy previously so she could donate her heart to him.

Johnboy wasn't his only visitor, apparently the FBI came by to inform him of some things. An agent, Erin Thatcher, informed him that Dean Giuseppe worked for the Talenti family and they were known for human trafficking.

"Did Kate mention any of this to you before?" Agent Thatcher asked.

"No," Luke said, sadly.

"Were you aware of any reason why Dean was determined to get Kate back?"

"No."

"Was there any chance that she was part of sex trafficking?"

"What?" Luke asked, angrily.

"Is there any reason you might have to believe she was *working* for them?" Agent Thatcher continued.

"I think that's enough questions," Johnboy jumped in.

"What the fuck is wrong with you people? My wife just died and now I have a constant reminder of her beating in my chest," Luke exclaimed.

"Sir, we're just doing our jobs," Agent Thatcher stated.

"Well, go fuck yourselves."

"I'm sorry, but we have a few more questions."

"Get the fuck out… Now!"

Agent Thatcher walked across the room and placed her business card on the table.

"Well, if you think of anything… give us a call," she said before leaving with her silent partner.

"Sorry about that, Luke," Johnboy apologized. "I didn't think they were going to ask questions. I thought they were going to provide some information."

"I don't… I just don't care anymore," Luke stated, before closing his eyes.

He had so much on his mind and didn't know how he could live with Kate's heart inside him and a baby girl he hoped and prayed made it through.

***

Even though he didn't care about his stardom, another perk about being a famous country singer, he was able to be in the same room with his baby girl so he could watch her sleep. Usually, the hospital didn't do such a thing, but they realized he really needed it.

As each day passed, he got stronger, as did with his daughter. Luke smiled as he knew she was a fighter like her mama. Eventually, they allowed him to hold her in his arms. He couldn't believe that the little squirming thing was his. Stroking her cheek with his finger, he smiled and laughed at how perfect she was.

"Just like your mama," he whispered.

***

"So, are you going to let anyone else hold her," Johnboy joked, carrying a bag for Luke.

Luke smiled, still holding his daughter in his arms as they walked toward their home. "No way, man, I helped make her," he said, with a laugh.

"Well, it's good to hear you laugh, again."

"It's probably just the medication," Luke said, sadly.

"I'm really sorry, Luke, I know it's not a good time, but maybe it's time to hire some help while you recuperate," Johnboy suggested.

"Yeah, I was thinking about that."

"Really?"

"Well, I figured I would need to give Adaline all my attention seeing as I'm the only one left to do so," Luke said, sadly, looking at the sleeping bundle in his arms.

He looked over his shoulder when he felt a hand on it.

"Bro, you're not alone," Johnboy said, with a smile.

"Thanks."

They continued inside the house as Luke's mind raced and his stomach twisted. He was hoping he was up to the job of being a single father.

***

Luke just stood there, looking at the casket. He still had trouble accepting all this was real. He didn't catch a single word that the preacher was saying, as all he could do was hope to wake up and find out this was nothing but a nightmare. But he knew his life wouldn't be the same. Fate was kind enough to bring his love back to his life but then rip her away from him in an instant. Swallowing hard, he tried to stay strong, but he could feel his body was ready to crumble at any moment. Closing his eyes, he tried his best to keep from breaking down as all their friends were gathered around to give their support.

How am I supposed to do this alone...

***

Luke groggily got up when he heard Adaline start to whimper, tripping over something in his room before making it to the crib. Picking up Adaline, her whimpering began to fade.

"It's okay, daddy's got you," he whispered, comforting her.

She began to squirm and whimper again. Luke started to hum a tune that popped in his head. Not realizing it, he started to sing it.

I am your lone star

You are what you are

In the night sky

I am your guide

To be home with me

Because of me

You are who you are

Because I'm your north star

I'm your world

You're my baby girl

I'll guide you home tonight

And keep your future bright…

As he finished the song, Adaline seemed content and fell right back to sleep.

"Sweet dreams, my little angel," Luke whispered, before planting a soft kiss on her forehead.

***

Luke stood behind a velvety curtain as he could hear the crowd out there. He was nervous as it had been a few years, but he figured he'd do this one tour in memory of Kate. While he was in his trailer the song *Alone* by I Prevail played. It made him sob for a while and delayed the concert while he could gathered himself again. He had been trying to hide his feelings about Kate as he still wasn't over the fact she was gone.

He almost broke down again, but collected himself so he could walk out on the stage. This was going to be a tough song, but he knew he had to sing it. He may not have been completely honest about his feelings, but at least he could sing about how he really felt.

The crowd cheered as he made his way to the microphone and put his hand up to help silence the crowd. Exhaling slowly, he knew it was going to be hard as his body began to shake from all of the emotions rushing through him.

"Thank you all for coming."

There were a few cheers and girls screaming that they loved him.

"This next song is dedicated to my only true love. It's called *Small Town Love*," he said, his voice shaky.

He started to strum the guitar trying to get himself ready to sing the song. He had sang it to himself many times before, but never in front of anyone else, even Adaline. Closing his eyes, he started to sing.

I could feel you with each beat of your heart

And it kills me so hard

Wishing you were here with me

And not there without me

That's the problem with a small town love

You always want more

And then you realize it's not there

And it's too late by then

There's a big world to explore

But it's not what it's all cracked up to be

That's the problem with small town love

She used to hold me

Now I hold her life

She used to look at me with love

Now I just turn to the sky

She used to say she loved me

Now I just say I miss her

She used to talk to me

Now she talks to angels

The day she slipped away

I'll never forget

I'll blame myself until the day

I can join her

I can still feel her

With every beat of my heart

I keep asking why

But it was meant to be this way

I always said your heart would be mine

And here we are today

It feels like you're singing with me

But again I know that cannot be

If it could be true

It would be both wonderful and beautiful

That's the problem with small town love…

Luke screwed his eyes as he bowed his head. He didn't hear anything as it was so quiet you could hear a pin drop. He wasn't going for a pity thing, but wanted to sing what he was feeling. Finally raising his head and looking out at the crowd that had tears in their eyes, he could feel tears flowing down his face.

"Thank you," he said, his voice cracking.

As he walked off the stage, he gave his guitar to the one guy who didn't say a word to him. He could tell a lot of people were in shock. He quickly wiped the tears from his face as he headed toward his trailer. Just then, something cheered up his heart in a flash.

"Daddy!" Adaline called out.

He smiled. "Adaline Katelyn," he called back.

He watched as she ran from CindyLou's side. He crouched down and caught her in his arms. She pulled out of his tight hug.

"Are you okay, Daddy," Adaline asked, wiping the remaining tear off his face.

"I'm fine, darling," he said, in a southern drawl.

Adaline giggled as he knew she loved it just as her mother when he talked like that. Looking up as CindyLou walked over.

"Hey, little bro, nice song," she said.

"Thanks," he said, sadly.

He was happy that CindyLou had survived the accident, but she lost half her left arm from it. He knew she was still tough with only half an arm, but he still wished he could have killed the bastard for everything he took from him. He returned his attention to Adaline and placed his cowboy hat on top of her head.

"Ready to go home, sweetie?" he asked.

"Yep," she said, excitedly.

Picking her up. "Okay, let's go home," he said, happily.

***

"Hey, sweetie, I have a surprise for you," Luke announced.

"What is it?" Adaline asked, running from CindyLou.

Luke put down a bundle of fur on the ground. The German Shepherd puppy bounced and barked as Adaline ran over and wrapped her arms around it.

"Oh, daddy, thank you, thank you," she said, excitedly.

Luke crouched down, patting the puppy. "So, what are you going to name it?" he asked.

"Hmmm... Charger," she announced.

Luke laughed. "Why Charger?" he asked.

"Because that was the kind of car you had," she said, with a big smile.

"Yeah, it was," he said, sadly.

***

Luke strummed the guitar with Adaline on his lap as he sat on the couch with his legs up on the coffee table.

"Daddy, can I hear mommy?" she asked.

"Sure you can," he said.

He wrapped an arm around her and pulled her close to his chest. After all these years, it still pained him that the only way their child would know her mother, was listening to her heart beating in his chest. He tried to stay strong and not break down in front of her, but today was another bad day as some of the memories of her started to fade. The Charger was totaled and with taking care of Adaline, he wouldn't be able have time to fix it up, so he eventually had to say goodbye to the memory.

Before he knew it, he felt Adaline's little hands on his face.

"Don't cry, Daddy, mommy would want us to be happy," she said.

Putting the guitar down, he wrapped her up in a tight hug.

"You're right, sweetie," he said, sadly.

***

"So, each day our daughter looks more like you... Oh my God, Kate, she's so perfect," Luke said, sadly, standing at Kate's grave.

He kept trying to wipe away the tears, but they kept flooding his eyes.

"I'm sorry, I know I shouldn't be angry, but I am... I'm angry with you for breaking your promise and leaving me again."

He crouched and played with pebbles on the ground.

"Damn it, Kate, how could you do this to me again and break my heart," he said, angrily.

Bowing his head. "I wish you were here... I don't think I could do this on my own."

Laughing and shaking his head. "You wouldn't believe the mumbo jumbo crap that CindyLou has been telling me because she took Psych 101 and believes I'm going through the stages of grief. Well, it's been four years and I'm still upset and angry with you. I mean...How could you do this to us," he said, before sobbing.

Leaning on his hands, he finally broke down.

"I miss you so much," he choked out between sobs.

***

"Hey, Adaline Katelyn, are you ready?" he called out from the kitchen.

When she didn't answer him, he walked out to find her in the living room, flipping through pages. As he got closer, he soon recognized the notebook she was going through.

"What are you doing, sweetie?" he asked, softly.

"I found this under the coffee table," she answered.

"Hey, go get your jacket on, okay?"

"Okay," she said, as she got up.

As Luke flipped through the notebook his hands shook. He didn't know how he'd never seen it laying around. He didn't even know when or how it got there. He then realized that probably Johnboy brought it back. He didn't know why, as it was just a painful reminder. As he continued to flip through the pages, his eyes filled with tears as he saw all the memories that he and Kate shared together. He spotted a few pages of songs and others were like scrapbook pages of photos and things to show an adventure they had. As he continued, he saw some of them were his bucket list. The notebook finally fell out of his hands because they were shaking so much. It opened to a page, as Luke tilted his head and squinted at it. He didn't know if he wanted to pick it up again and read what was on the page which had a picture of him and Kate when they went out to dinner at the fancy restaurant.

He slowly picked up the notebook, believing it would burn him if he touched it. As his eyes started to read the entry, he was surprised by what he was reading.

Dear Luke,

If you're reading this, it must mean I didn't make it. I'm hoping that our baby girl at least made it so you wouldn't be alone. I hate that it had to end like this, but I don't want you to be sad for me. I want you to move on and live your life like we did together. Keep going on adventures and singing your heart out. Remember, you were my lone star in my night sky that guided me home. I am and will always be grateful for everything you have done for me and the life we had. But now, it's time for you to move on and be happy. So, please go live your life and one day we'll be reunited.

Love Always,

Kate

After finishing reading the entry, Luke held the notebook close to his chest as the tears fell. He didn't expect this to happen, but a smile slowly formed on his face.

"Thank you, Kate," he whispered to himself.

"Daddy, I'm ready," Adaline said, cheerfully.

Quickly wiping away his tears, he placed the notebook on the coffee table and walked over to Adaline. Holding his hand out, she took it as they went outside the house.

"Come on, Charger," Adaline called out.

The puppy barked and ran after them. Luke smiled as he felt better after reading Kate's entry. He knew he had to stop staying in the past and move on as his daughter needed him to move on, with her.

CHAPTER NINE

Luke was fixing the tractor as Adaline sat on a stool.

"Wrench," he requested.

"Wrench," she repeated, and handed him the tool.

He smiled over at her as she smiled back. She had grease smeared on her face just like him, and he could tell she was becoming more like her mama every day. Earlier, he had found her rolling around in the mud with the piglets after chasing them around. He couldn't help but laugh as he knew she was a pure country girl.

The days were getting better as he had Adaline by his side every day. She would help him with a lot of things on the farm and had named all the animals. His favorite was when she named a bull Twinkle Toes. He couldn't help but laugh. She had a sense of adventure and saw the good in the world, just like her mama. Every day he was thankful that he had been able to get a heart and watch her grow up.

"Hey, little bro, ready to go," CindyLou called out, walking over to them.

"Yep, just one more bolt."

"Aunt C," Adaline yelled, as she got down and ran over to her.

"Ah, there's my cutie betonies," CindyLou said.

Luke watched with a big smile as CindyLou acted as if she didn't need most of her left arm anyway, as she was able to pick up Adaline fine with her right arm.

I guess when life gives you lemons, you make lemonade…

***

Luke was nervous when CindyLou insisted on driving his pickup truck. Last time he let someone drive his vehicle they ended up being taken away from him. Eventually, his nervousness went away as Adaline started to sing *Two Princes* by Spin Doctors and Luke joined in. As they continued to sing with the radio, Luke felt CindyLou slowing the truck and pulling in somewhere. When he looked, he felt his heart racing as it was very familiar.

"C, what are we doing here?" he asked, sternly.

"Getting gas."

"Of all places, you decided this would be the place to get gas?"

"Oh, Luke, you need to get over your aversion to this place," she said, waving her hand.

She pulled up at the gas pump as Luke tried to calm his nerves. Looking out the window, he recognized the place as the gas station he found Kate stranded at. He was hoping to avoid the place at all cost, but apparently his sister was being thick-skulled again.

As she got out, she looked over at Luke.

"Hey, little bro, why don't you be a dear and go grab a snack for Adaline inside?"

"I'd prefer not to."

"Please, Daddy," Adaline pleaded.

"Fine," he said, giving in.

Getting out and walking toward the gas station, he tried not to look in the direction where he spotted Kate.

"Howdy, cowboy, can I get a lift?" a female voice called out.

Luke stopped and slowly turned his head, not believing he had heard the voice. Blinking his eyes a few times before rubbing them, he thought he must have finally lost it. A girl was standing there with her thumb out that almost looked like Kate, the only difference, the dark brown in her hair was fading to her natural hair color. He slowly started to walk toward her, still unsure that she was real.

"Katelyn?" he questioned, not removing his eyes from her.

"Hey there, cowboy, what does a girl have to do to get the man she left behind back into her life?" Kate teased.

Wrapping his arms around her tightly. "Nothing," he said.

He quickly pulled away and looked back as his pickup truck drove away. He didn't know what his sister was up to and wouldn't doubt that she had this planned, but was surprised she had managed to keep the secret.

"Well, it looks like we're both looking for a ride," Kate joked.

"Yeah, I guess," he said, confusion in his voice.

He became concerned when a 2013 Charger slowed to a stop next to them. He watched as Johnboy got out of it with a big smile on his face. He tossed the keys, and Kate caught them. Luke's pickup truck stopped by Johnboy and he got in, leaving Luke and Kate with the Charger.

"So, let's catch up," Kate said, before tossing the keys to Luke.

Luke was still in shock at all this as he stared down at the keys in his hands, and the only way he came out of it was when Kate leaned in on her tipsy toes to whisper in his ear.

"Let's make it like old times."

"Don't need to tell me twice," he said, as he rushed to get in the car.

Kate laughed as they drove away, and he smiled back at her. It was like old times, but in a different year of a Charger.

***

As they lay naked in bed together after physically catching up, Luke was still struggling with the fact that she was back in his life.

"So, can you please tell me what's going on?" he begged.

Stroking his face. "I'm so sorry, Luke, for putting you through this."

"It was tough, but thankfully I had Adaline to remind what was worth living for," he said.

"I'm so glad she made it through. It was touch and go there for a while."

"So, whose heart do I have if it isn't yours?"

"While you were unconscious, I had an emergency C-section for Adaline then had to have emergency surgery myself. They weren't sure if I was going to make it. Then, after the surgery, the FBI showed up. They were questioning me about Dean and I realized what they were after. So, I told them if they wanted my help they would need to do a few things for me. One was for you to get a heart, so our baby girl wouldn't be alone in this world. Two, they would have to pretend I was dead so that the Talenti family wouldn't come after you guys."

"I wish you hadn't done that, babe, I was so fucked up after I thought you were dead."

"I'm sorry, Luke, but I couldn't chance them coming after you guys, so I had to go into witness protection. I wanted you to have a life and not be imprisoned as I was. You wouldn't believe how hard it was not to contact you guys. I missed you so much, Luke, especially when I looked up at the night sky."

"So, why did the FBI want you?"

"Well they told me if I didn't leave when I did, then Dean was going to sell me to some guy because he had grown tired of me and I was no longer the perfect advertisement. I thought I was arm candy, but I found out I was just an advertisement piece for the Talenti family's business of human trafficking."

"Oh my God, Kate… that's horrible…" Luke said, shocked.

"It was, but I had a backup plan. As I played his arm candy, Dean thought I was stupid and didn't think twice about me being around some things I probably shouldn't have seen. I was able to memorize numbers and faces from the business, just in case I needed it. Good thing I did, or the FBI wouldn't have been able to put away Dean, or the Talentis."

He pulled her tight against him. "Please, babe, don't ever do that again," he begged.

"I won't and I'm so sorry, Luke. I wish it could have gone a different way."

He started to nibble along her jawline as he missed feeling her warm body against his in this bed. As things started to heat up, he heard some small footsteps make their way toward the bedroom. He quickly pulled away and put on some pajama bottoms as Kate slipped on one of his shirts and boxers. The door slowly opened, and Adaline ran in.

"Daddy!" she screamed.

He caught her in his arms as she got on the bed and jumped. "Boy, little one, are you learning from your aunt?" he teased.

"Aunt C told me it would be funny to run in here."

Luke rolled his eyes. "Aunt C and I are going to have a talk about what's funny."

"Hi honey," Kate said.

Luke could see that Adaline seemed to recognize Kate's voice, but still wasn't sure.

"Hey, sweetie, this is your mommy," he announced.

Excitement built up on her face as she jumped over into Kate's open arms.

"Mommy, where have you been? Daddy said you were alive inside him."

"I know I'll always be in his heart, but it's a very long story that I think we'll keep for another day," Kate said, looking over at Luke, who smiled his approval.

Charger started to bark and ran in to join in the family reunion. Kate laughed as he tried licking her face. Luke still couldn't believe how his life had changed. He was hoping he wasn't going to wake up from this if it were a dream.

***

As Luke and Kate finished their song on stage, the crowd cheered and clapped. Luke's smile grew as he looked at Kate and realized they had finally reached their dream of being country singers.

"Ready to sing another song?"

"With you, babe, of course," he said.

He strummed his guitar as Kate hummed along with it and started to sing.

You are my lone star...

ABOUT THE AUTHOR

Dawn L. Lubertowicz spent most of her childhood traveling the world with her family, where she learned all of the different cultures. She was born in Denver, Colorado and never stopped moving until 1990 when the Persian Gulf War forced her, her mother and her older sister to move back to the United States. She finally settled down in a small town, Tunkhannock with her husband, Jason and their "furry children", Gremlin, Storm, Ashes and Fudge. She went to college and graduated with a bachelor degree in psychology, minor in criminal justice, and a certificate in Forensic Science.

Dawn L. Lubertowicz brings great sense of humor and great personalities to each of her characters in all her stories. The combination of her endless imagination and witty personality, will keep you reading. Each story, you will feel the pain, happiness, sadness and humor. As you fall in love with the characters you will feel what they're feeling along the way.

www.ingramcontent.com/pod-product-compliance
Lightning Source LLC
Chambersburg PA
CBHW070613120726
47909CB00004B/1211